# SHADOWS OF WAR

*A Novel*
*Sequel to Shadows of Trust*

By Jasmine Deatherage

# OUTLINE

## ACT I: THE STORM GATHERS

## ACT II: INTO THE SHADOWS

## ACT III: THE HUNT

## ACT IV: THE FINAL RECKONING

# ACT I: THE STORM GATHERS

# Chapter 1: Shattered Peace

The salt-laced air of Whidbey Island was a balm to Marcus Sterling's soul. Three years had passed since the ghosts of his past had nearly consumed him, three years since he had been forced to resurrect the man he had tried to bury: Phoenix, the CIA operative who had walked through the world's darkest shadows. Now, those shadows seemed a lifetime away.

His home, a modern structure of glass and cedar, clung to a bluff overlooking the Puget Sound. It was a fortress of peace, a sanctuary he had built with his wife, Tori, a woman whose love had been his anchor in the storm. Together, they had created a life here, a world away from the lies and violence that had once defined him.

He watched from the deck as Tori and Elena, his daughter, walked along the private beach below. Elena, a young woman forged in the crucible of her own tragic past, had come into their lives like a whirlwind, a living reminder of a mission gone wrong and a promise he had unknowingly made. She was a mirror of him in so many ways—her sharp instincts, her quiet intensity, the shadows that still flickered in her eyes. But here, in the gentle rhythm of the waves and the steadfast warmth of Tori's love, she was healing. They all were.

"I could get used to this," Tori said, her voice a soft melody as she joined him on the deck, wrapping her arms around his waist. She rested her head on his shoulder, her gaze following his to the beach where Elena was skipping stones across the water's surface.

"I think I already have," Marcus replied, his voice a low rumble. He pressed a kiss to her temple, the familiar scent of her hair a comfort. "It's a good life."

"The best," she whispered, her hand finding his. Their fingers intertwined, a silent testament to the battles they had fought and won together. The scars remained, both seen and unseen, but they were a part of their story, a map of their journey to this moment of quiet serenity.

But the quiet was a fragile thing, a delicate bubble he knew could burst at any moment. The world he had left behind was not one to forgive or forget. It was a world of whispers and shadows, of old debts and new threats. And as much as he wished it were not so, he knew that a man like him could never truly be free.

The shrill ring of his phone shattered the peace. It was a sound he had not heard in three years, a sound that sent a jolt of ice through his veins. It was a dedicated line, a ghost from his past he had been assured would remain silent. He pulled away from Tori, his movements stiff, his eyes locking onto the unfamiliar number on the screen.

"Don't," Tori pleaded, her voice barely a whisper. She knew what that phone represented, the world it could drag him back into. "Marcus, please."

He looked at her, his heart aching at the fear in her eyes. But he had to answer. He had to know. With a deep breath, he swiped the screen, his voice a low, steady command. "This is Sterling."

The voice on the other end was clipped, professional, a voice he recognized from a lifetime ago. Colonel Jackson, his former handler, a man who had been both his mentor and his tormentor. "Phoenix," Jackson said, the name a punch to the gut. "We have a situation."

Marcus's blood ran cold. He turned away from Tori, his back to the life he had built, his gaze fixed on the turbulent waters of the Sound. "I'm not Phoenix anymore, Jackson. You know that."

"The world doesn't care what you call yourself," Jackson replied, his voice grim. "A U.S. naval carrier, the *USS Roosevelt*, was just hit in the Caribbean. A tactical nuclear device. The fleet is in chaos. We're looking at a ghost, Phoenix. No one is claiming responsibility. No one has the resources. Except..."

Jackson didn't need to finish the sentence. Marcus knew. The Syndicate. A name whispered in the darkest corners of the intelligence community, a coalition of cartels, rogue agents, and arms dealers who had been quietly amassing power for years. They were the boogeymen of the new world order, a threat he had warned his superiors about before he had walked away.

"I'm out, Jackson," Marcus said, his voice a low growl. But the words felt hollow, a lie he was telling himself. He could already feel the old instincts stirring, the familiar weight of the world settling on his shoulders.

"Are you?" Jackson countered, his voice a sharp blade. "This isn't just a mission, Phoenix. This is the beginning of a new kind of war. And you are the only one who knows how to fight it."

The line went dead, but the silence that followed was deafening. Marcus stood there, the phone in his hand, the weight of Jackson's words pressing down on him. He looked at his reflection in the glass of the deck door, and for a moment, he did not see Marcus Sterling, the husband, the father. He saw Phoenix, the man he had tried to leave behind, the man the world would not let him forget.

He turned to face Tori, his expression a mask of grim resolve. She already knew. She could see it in his eyes, in the way he held himself, the subtle shift from the man she loved to the weapon he had been trained to be.

"I have to go," he said, his voice heavy with the weight of the words. "I have to end this. For good."

Her eyes filled with tears, but she did not argue. She knew him, knew the man he was, the man he had to be. She simply nodded, her hand reaching for his, her touch a silent promise of her love, her strength, her unwavering support.

Down on the beach, Elena had stopped skipping stones. She was looking up at the house, her expression a mirror of her father's. She knew, too. The shadows had found them again. And this time, they would not be so easily banished.

The storm had come to Whidbey Island. And Phoenix was the only one who could walk into its heart and survive.

The morning after the call from Colonel Jackson, Marcus found himself standing at the edge of the bluff, watching the sun rise over the Puget Sound. The sky was a canvas of orange and pink, a masterpiece of nature that seemed to mock the turmoil in his heart. He had not slept. The words of his former handler echoed in his mind, a relentless drumbeat that would not be silenced.

A tactical nuclear device. The *USS Roosevelt*. The Syndicate.

IIe had spent years trying to bury Phoenix, to become the man he saw in Tori's eyes—a husband, a father, a man of peace. But the world had a way of pulling him back, of reminding him that some debts could never be paid, some shadows could never be escaped.

He heard her footsteps before he saw her. Tori moved with a quiet grace, her presence a warmth that cut through the morning chill. She stood beside him, her hand finding his, her fingers intertwining with his own.

"You're going, aren't you?" she asked, her voice a soft whisper. There was no accusation in her tone, only a quiet resignation, a understanding that had been forged in the fires of their shared past.

"I don't have a choice," he replied, his voice a low rumble. "If what Jackson says is true, if The Syndicate is behind this… they won't stop with one attack. They'll keep pushing until the world burns."

"And you're the only one who can stop them?" There was a hint of bitterness in her voice, a pain that he knew he had caused.

He turned to face her, his hands cupping her face, his eyes searching hers. "I'm the only one who knows how they think, how they operate. I helped build the intelligence that was supposed to stop them. And I walked away. This is my responsibility, Tori. My failure."

She closed her eyes, a single tear tracing a path down her cheek. "I knew this day would come," she whispered. "I just hoped… I hoped we would have more time."

He pulled her into his arms, holding her tight, the scent of her hair a familiar comfort. "I will come back to you," he promised, his voice a fierce vow. "I will always come back to you."

They stood there, on the edge of the bluff, as the sun rose over the Sound, two souls clinging to each other in the face of the coming storm. The weight of peace was a heavy one, and it was about to be shattered.

# Chapter 2: The Call to Arms

The silence in the house was a heavy shroud, a stark contrast to the idyllic peace of moments before. Tori's hand was a warm anchor in the cold sea of Marcus's thoughts, her touch a reminder of everything he stood to lose. He looked at her, his heart a leaden weight in his chest. "I'm sorry," he whispered, the words inadequate, a pale shadow of the apology he owed her.

"Don't be," she replied, her voice steady despite the tears that shimmered in her eyes. "Just... come back to me. To us."

He pulled her into his arms, holding her tight, the scent of her hair a familiar comfort in a world that had suddenly become alien and hostile. "Always," he promised, his voice a low growl. "I will always come back to you."

He released her, his gaze shifting to the beach where Elena was now walking towards the house, her steps measured, her expression a mask of grim understanding. She had seen the change in him, the subtle shift from father to soldier. She had lived in the shadows long enough to recognize their touch.

"I need to make a call," Marcus said, his voice clipped, professional. He walked into his study, the one room in the house that was a fortress within a fortress, a place where the ghosts of his past were allowed to whisper. He sat behind his desk, the smooth, cool surface of the wood a stark contrast to the turmoil in his mind. He pulled out a satellite phone, a relic from his former life he had hoped he would never have to use again. He punched in a number, the sequence of digits a familiar rhythm in his muscle memory.

The voice that answered was a voice he had not heard in three years, a voice that had once been his lifeline in the darkest corners of the world. "Sarah," he said, his voice a low rumble. "It's me."

There was a moment of silence on the other end of the line, then a sharp intake of breath. "Marcus?" Sarah's voice was a mixture of shock and relief. "I thought... I thought you were out."

"I was," he replied, his voice grim. "But something's happened. Something big."

He told her everything, his words a torrent of information, a grim tapestry of nuclear threats and shadowy syndicates. Sarah listened, her silence a testament to her professionalism, her occasional questions sharp, insightful, a reminder of why she had been the best analyst the CIA had ever had.

"The Syndicate," she said, her voice a low whisper when he had finished. "I've heard the whispers, Marcus. But I never thought... I never thought they had this kind of power."

"They do," he replied, his voice a low growl. "And they're just getting started."

"What do you need?" she asked, her voice steady, professional. She was already in, already a part of the mission. He knew she would be. They were family, bound by the secrets they shared, the battles they had fought together.

"I need a team," he said, his voice a low command. "The old team. The ones who can walk in the shadows without leaving a trace."

"They're scattered, Marcus," she replied, her voice a low whisper. "Some of them are dead. Some of them are ghosts."

"Find them," he said, his voice a low growl. "The ones who are still alive. The ones who can still fight. We're getting the band back together, Sarah. One last time."

He ended the call, the weight of his words hanging in the air. He looked at the photo on his desk, a picture of him and Tori on their wedding day, their faces a portrait of hope and happiness. He had fought for that life, had bled for it. And now, he would have to fight for it again.

He walked out of the study, his steps heavy, his heart a battlefield of conflicting emotions. Tori was waiting for him in the living room, her expression a mixture of fear and resolve. Elena was standing beside her, her arms crossed, her eyes a reflection of her father's grim determination.

"I'm going with you," Elena said, her voice a low, steady command. It was not a request. It was a statement of fact.

"No," Marcus replied, his voice a low growl. "It's too dangerous."

"I'm not a child anymore, Dad," she said, her voice a sharp blade. "I can handle myself. You know I can."

He looked at her, his daughter, a young woman who had been forged in the crucible of violence and loss. He saw the strength in her eyes, the fire in her soul. He saw himself. And he knew, with a sinking heart, that he could not stop her.

"She's right, Marcus," Tori said, her voice a soft melody. "She's a part of this, whether we like it or not. And she's safer with you than she is without you."

He looked at them, his family, his world. He had tried to build a fortress of peace, a sanctuary from the shadows. But the shadows had found them anyway. And now, they would have to walk into the heart of the storm together.

"Alright," he said, his voice a low whisper. "We do this together."

He pulled them into his arms, holding them tight, the three of them a small island of love and resolve in a world that had suddenly become a battlefield. The call to arms had been answered. And the Sterling family, a family forged in the crucible of secrets and lies, would face the coming storm together.

The journey to the secure facility in Virginia was a descent into a world Marcus had tried to forget. The sterile corridors, the hushed voices, the constant hum of electronic surveillance—it was a world of shadows and secrets, a world where trust was a currency that was always in short supply.

Colonel Jackson was waiting for him in a secure briefing room, a space that was designed to be impenetrable to the outside world. He was an older man now, his hair a steel gray, his face a map of the battles he had fought. But his eyes were the same—sharp, calculating, a predator's gaze that missed nothing.

"Phoenix," Jackson said, his voice a low rumble. "It's been a long time."

"Not long enough," Marcus replied, his voice a cold edge. He took a seat across from Jackson, his posture a study in controlled tension. "Tell me everything."

Jackson slid a folder across the table, a collection of photographs and intelligence reports that painted a picture of a world on the brink of chaos. The attack on the *USS Roosevelt* was just the beginning. The Syndicate had been quietly building their power for years, a shadow empire that had infiltrated governments, corporations, and criminal organizations around the world.

"They're not just a criminal organization," Jackson explained, his voice grim. "They're a new kind of threat, a hybrid entity that operates like a state but with none of the accountability. They have the resources of a superpower and the ruthlessness of a terrorist cell."

Marcus studied the photographs, his mind a whirlwind of analysis. He recognized some of the faces—former colleagues, old enemies, ghosts from his past who had been consumed by the darkness. "Who's leading them?" he asked, his voice a low growl.

"We don't know," Jackson admitted, his voice a frustrated sigh. "They call him The Serpent, but that's just a codename. He's a ghost, a man with no face, no past, no identity. He's the one who's pulling the strings, the one who's orchestrating this new world order."

Marcus felt a chill run down his spine. The Serpent. It was a name he had heard before, a whisper in the darkest corners of the intelligence community. He had dismissed it as a myth, a boogeyman story told to scare new recruits. But now, it seemed, the myth was real.

"What do you need from me?" Marcus asked, his voice a low command.

"I need you to do what you do best," Jackson replied, his voice a grim determination. "I need you to hunt."

# Chapter 3: Shadows of the Past

The decision to bring Elena into the fold was a heavy one, a choice that sat like a stone in Marcus's gut. He had spent the last three years trying to shield her from the world he had left behind, a world of violence and betrayal, a world that had already taken so much from her. But he also knew that she was no longer the fragile girl he had rescued from the clutches of her grandfather. She was a survivor, a warrior, a woman who had been forged in the crucible of her own tragic past.

He found her in the gym, a state-of-the-art facility he had built in the basement of their home. She was a blur of motion, her movements a graceful dance of violence as she worked the heavy bag. Her fists were a blur, her feet a whirlwind of motion, her expression a mask of grim concentration. She was her father's daughter, a weapon in her own right.

"I need to know you're ready for this, Elena," he said, his voice a low rumble. He stood in the doorway, his arms crossed, his gaze fixed on her.

She stopped, her chest heaving, her face flushed with exertion. She turned to face him, her eyes a reflection of his own. "I was born ready for this, Dad," she said, her voice a low, steady command.

He walked towards her, his steps measured, his expression a mixture of pride and fear. "This isn't a game, Elena," he said, his voice a low growl. "This is real. The people we're going up against... they're not like anyone you've ever faced before."

"I know," she replied, her voice a low whisper. "But I'm not afraid."

"You should be," he said, his voice a sharp blade. "Fear keeps you alive."

He began to spar with her, their movements a blur of motion, a dance of violence that was both beautiful and terrifying. He was testing her, pushing her, trying to find her limits. But she met him at every turn, her movements a mirror of his own, her instincts as sharp as a razor's edge.

He saw the ghosts of her past in her eyes, the shadows of the trauma she had endured. But he also saw a strength, a resilience, a fire that burned brighter than any darkness. She was not just a survivor. She was a warrior.

"You're ready," he said, his voice a low whisper when they had finished. He pulled her into his arms, holding her tight, the father in him warring with the soldier. "But I still don't like it."

"I know," she replied, her voice a soft melody. "But we do this together. Remember?"

He nodded, his heart a battlefield of conflicting emotions. He had tried to shield her from his world, but his world had found her anyway. And now, they would have to walk into the shadows together.

Later that night, he found Tori in their bedroom, her expression a mixture of fear and resolve. She was packing a bag for him, her movements a study in quiet efficiency. She had been through this before, had lived through the long nights of waiting, the gnawing fear of the unknown. But this time was different. This time, their daughter was walking into the storm with him.

"I'm scared, Marcus," she said, her voice a low whisper. She stopped packing, her hands trembling. "I'm so scared."

He pulled her into his arms, holding her tight, his own fear a cold knot in his stomach. "I know," he said, his voice a low rumble. "But we're going to be okay. We're going to come back. All of us."

"You promise?" she asked, her voice a child's plea.

"I promise," he replied, his voice a low, steady command. It was a promise he knew he might not be able to keep, a promise that was a fragile shield against the darkness that was coming. But it was a promise he had to make, a promise he had to believe in.

He held her for a long time, the two of them a small island of love and hope in a world that was teetering on the brink of chaos. The shadows of the past had returned, and they were longer and darker than ever before. But this time, he was not alone. He had his family, his team, his reason to fight. And that, he knew, was a weapon more powerful than any gun, any bomb, any army.

Elena Sterling was not a woman who was easily frightened. She had survived horrors that would have broken most people, had been forged in a crucible of violence and betrayal. But the news of her father's return to the world of shadows filled her with a cold, creeping dread.

She found him in the gym, the one room in the house that was still a fortress, a space where he could shed the mask of the peaceful husband and father and become the warrior he had always been. He was working the heavy bag, his movements a blur of controlled violence, his breath a steady rhythm.

"You're going after them," she said, her voice a flat statement. It was not a question.

He stopped, his chest heaving, his eyes meeting hers. "I have to," he replied, his voice a low rumble. "They're a threat to everything we've built. To you. To Tori. To the world."

"Then I'm coming with you," she said, her voice a fierce determination.

He shook his head, his expression a mixture of pride and fear. "No. This is my fight, Elena. My responsibility."

"It's my fight too," she countered, her voice rising. "They're a part of my past, too. The people who made me, who trained me, who turned me into a weapon—they're all connected to The Syndicate. I have a right to be a part of this."

He saw the fire in her eyes, the same fire that burned in his own. She was his daughter, a warrior in her own right, a woman who had earned the right to stand beside him. He knew he could not protect her by keeping her away. He could only protect her by fighting alongside her.

"Alright," he said, a reluctant pride in his voice. "But you follow my lead. We do this together, as a family."

She nodded, a silent agreement passing between them. The daughter's burden was a heavy one, but she was ready to carry it. She was a Sterling, a warrior, a ghost. And she would not be denied.

# Chapter 4: The Difficult Conversation

The next morning, the house was a hive of activity. Sarah had arrived, her presence a whirlwind of energy and efficiency. She had set up a command center in the study, her fingers a blur on the keyboard as she coordinated with the scattered members of their old team. The ghosts were coming back, one by one, drawn by the call to arms, by the loyalty they still felt to the man who had led them through the darkest corners of the world.

Marcus watched her work, a sense of grim satisfaction settling in his gut. Sarah was the best, a digital ghost who could walk through firewalls and dance through encrypted networks without leaving a trace. She was the heart of their operation, the one who would keep them alive in the digital battlefield that was to come.

But there was one more conversation he had to have, a conversation he had been dreading. He found Tori in the kitchen, her expression a mask of quiet resolve. She was making breakfast, her movements a study in forced normalcy. But he could see the tension in her shoulders, the fear in her eyes.

"We need to talk," he said, his voice a low rumble. He sat at the kitchen island, his gaze fixed on her.

She stopped what she was doing, her hands trembling. She turned to face him, her eyes a reflection of his own. "I know," she said, her voice a low whisper.

"This is going to be different, Tori," he said, his voice a low growl. "This isn't just a mission. This is a war. And it's a war we might not win."

"I know that, Marcus," she replied, her voice a soft melody. "But I also know you. I know you have to do this. I know you have to try."

"But what if I don't come back?" he asked, his voice a raw whisper. The question hung in the air between them, a heavy shroud of fear and uncertainty.

She walked towards him, her steps measured, her expression a mixture of love and resolve. She took his hands in hers, her touch a warm anchor in the cold sea of his thoughts. "Then you will have died fighting for what you believe in," she said, her voice a steady command. "You will have died protecting your family, your country, the world. And there is no greater honor than that."

He looked at her, his heart aching at the strength in her eyes, the unwavering love in her soul. She was his rock, his anchor, his reason to fight. And he knew, with a certainty that was as deep and as vast as the ocean, that he would do whatever it took to come back to her.

"I love you," he said, his voice a low whisper. He pulled her into his arms, holding her tight, the scent of her hair a familiar comfort in a world that had suddenly become alien and hostile.

"I love you, too," she replied, her voice a soft melody. "Now go. Go and be the man you were always meant to be."

He released her, his gaze shifting to the doorway where Elena was standing, her expression a mixture of pride and fear. She had heard everything, had witnessed the raw emotion of their conversation. She walked towards them, her steps measured, her expression a mask of grim resolve.

"We're in this together, Dad," she said, her voice a low, steady command. "We fight together. We win together. Or we die together."

He looked at them, his family, his world. He had tried to build a fortress of peace, a sanctuary from the shadows. But the shadows had found them anyway. And now, they would have to walk into the heart of the storm together.

"Together," he said, his voice a low whisper. He pulled them into his arms, holding them tight, the three of them a small island of love and resolve in a world that was teetering on the brink of chaos. The difficult conversation was over. The battle lines had been drawn. And the Sterling family, a family forged in the crucible of secrets and lies, would face the coming storm together.

The conversation with Tori was the hardest one Marcus had ever had. He sat across from her in their living room, the space that had been their sanctuary, their refuge from the world. Now, it felt like a confessional, a place where he had to lay bare the secrets he had kept hidden for so long.

"There are things about my past that I never told you," he began, his voice a low, hesitant rumble. "Things I was ashamed of, things I thought I could bury and forget."

Tori's expression was a mask of calm, but he could see the storm brewing in her eyes. "Tell me," she said, her voice a steady command.

He told her about The Syndicate, about the intelligence he had gathered, the warnings he had given that had been ignored. He told her about the missions he had run, the lives he had taken, the compromises he had made in the name of national security. He told her about the man he had been, the ghost who had walked through the world's darkest shadows.

"I thought I could leave it all behind," he said, his voice a hoarse whisper. "I thought I could become someone new, someone worthy of you. But the past has a way of catching up, Tori. And now, it's threatening everything we've built."

She was silent for a long moment, her gaze fixed on some distant point. When she finally spoke, her voice was a mixture of pain and resolve. "I knew you had secrets, Marcus. I knew there were parts of your past you couldn't share. But I married you, all of you, the light and the dark. And I'm not going to abandon you now."

She reached across the space between them, her hand finding his. "We face this together," she said, her voice a fierce vow. "As a family."

The weight of secrets was a heavy one, but in that moment, Marcus felt it lift, just a little. He was not alone. He had Tori, he had Elena, he had a family that was willing to walk into the darkness with him. And that, he knew, was the greatest strength of all.

# Chapter 5: Assembling the Team

The ghosts began to arrive, one by one, drawn from the shadows by the call of their former leader. They were a motley crew, a collection of misfits and outcasts, the forgotten soldiers of a secret war. They were the ones who had walked through the world's darkest corners, the ones who had done the dirty work that no one else would do. They were Phoenix's team.

First came Javier, a wiry Colombian with a penchant for explosives and a grin that could charm the devil himself. He had been a ghost for five years, living a quiet life in the mountains of his homeland. But when the call came, he had not hesitated. He owed Marcus his life, a debt he was more than willing to repay.

Next was Anya, a former Mossad agent with a mind as sharp as a razor and a body that was a weapon in its own right. She had been working as a freelance security consultant in Tel Aviv, her skills for hire to the highest bidder. But her loyalty to Marcus ran deeper than any paycheck. She was in.

Then came Kenji, a Japanese hacker who could dance through firewalls and bend the digital world to his will. He had been living off the grid, a digital ghost who had erased his own existence. But Sarah had found him, had pulled him back from the brink of oblivion. He was a reluctant soldier, a man who had seen too much of the darkness. But he could not refuse the call. Not when the world was at stake.

They gathered in the study, a room that had become the war room of their new mission. The air was thick with tension, with the unspoken memories of battles fought and comrades lost. They were older now, their faces etched with the lines of time and experience. But the fire was still in their eyes, the warrior's spirit still burning bright.

Marcus stood before them, his presence a commanding force, the leader they had followed into the heart of the storm time and time again. He looked at them, his team, his family. He saw the ghosts of their past in their eyes, the shadows of the battles they had fought together. But he also saw a strength, a resilience, a loyalty that had not faded with time.

"Welcome back," he said, his voice a low rumble. "I wish it were under better circumstances."

"It always is, boss," Javier said, his grin a flash of white in the dim light of the room. "Where's the fire?"

Marcus told them everything, his words a grim tapestry of nuclear threats and shadowy syndicates. They listened, their expressions a mixture of shock and resolve. They had seen the darkness, had walked through the fire. But this was different. This was a new kind of war, a war that threatened to consume the world.

"The Syndicate," Anya said, her voice a low whisper when he had finished. "I've heard the whispers. But I never thought... I never thought they were real."

"They're real," Marcus replied, his voice a low growl. "And they're just getting started."

"So what's the plan?" Kenji asked, his voice a low murmur. He was already at the keyboard, his fingers a blur as he danced through the digital world.

"The plan is simple," Marcus said, his voice a low command. "We find them. We stop them. And we make sure they can never threaten anyone ever again."

He looked at them, his team, his family. He saw the fear in their eyes, the uncertainty. But he also saw a resolve, a determination, a loyalty that was as strong as steel. They were in. All of them.

"One last dance with the devil," Javier said, his grin a flash of white. "I'm in."

"For you, Marcus," Anya said, her voice a low whisper. "Anything."

"Let's get to work," Kenji said, his voice a low murmur. He had already found a thread, a digital breadcrumb that could lead them to the heart of the beast.

Marcus looked at them, a sense of grim satisfaction settling in his gut. The ghosts had returned. The team was back together. And the world, whether it knew it or not, had a fighting chance.

The assembly of the team was a reunion of ghosts, a gathering of warriors who had been scattered to the four corners of the earth. They came at Marcus's call, a summons that was both a request and a command. They were the best of the best, a collection of specialists who had walked through the world's darkest corners and had emerged, scarred but unbroken.

Javier, the explosives expert, arrived first. He was a bear of a man, his grin a flash of white against his dark skin. He had been Marcus's partner on a dozen missions, a man whose loyalty was as unshakable as his nerve. He greeted Marcus with a bone-crushing hug, his laughter a booming echo in the quiet of the house.

"Phoenix, you old ghost," Javier said, his voice a warm rumble. "I thought you were done with this life."

"So did I," Marcus replied, a wry smile on his face. "But the world had other plans."

Anya, the former Mossad agent, arrived next. She was a woman of few words, her presence a quiet intensity that filled the room. She had been Marcus's shadow on some of his most dangerous missions, a woman who could kill with a touch, a whisper, a glance. She nodded at Marcus, a silent acknowledgment of the bond they shared.

Kenji and Sarah, the digital ghosts, were already there, their virtual presence a constant hum in the background. They were the eyes and ears of the operation, the ones who would guide the team through the digital battlefield. They were a team of hunters, a pair of ghosts who could tear down the walls of any fortress.

They gathered in the war room, a space that had been transformed into a command center. The walls were covered with maps and photographs, a visual representation of the enemy they were about to face. The mood was grim, the air thick with the unspoken understanding that they were about to walk into the lion's den.

"The Syndicate is a new kind of threat," Marcus began, his voice a low command. "They're not just criminals. They're a shadow government, a coalition of the world's most dangerous players. And they're planning something big."

He laid out the intelligence, the pieces of the puzzle that they had gathered. The attack on the *USS Roosevelt* was just the beginning. The Syndicate was planning a series of coordinated strikes, a campaign of terror that would destabilize the global order and allow them to seize power.

"Our mission is simple," Marcus concluded, his voice a grim determination. "We find them. We stop them. And we bring them down."

The call to arms had been answered. The ghosts were ready. The hunt was about to begin.

# Chapter 6: The Shadow Network

The study was a symphony of controlled chaos, a whirlwind of digital ghosts and whispered secrets. Kenji was a maestro at the keyboard, his fingers a blur as he conducted a symphony of data, his eyes a reflection of the digital world he was navigating. Sarah was his partner in crime, her own skills a perfect complement to his, the two of them a formidable force in the digital battlefield.

They were hunting for a ghost, a digital phantom who had left no trace, no breadcrumbs, no clues. The attack on the *USS Roosevelt* had been a masterpiece of misdirection, a digital sleight of hand that had left the world's intelligence agencies blind and bewildered. But Kenji and Sarah were not just analysts. They were artists. And they were beginning to see the brushstrokes of the master who had painted this canvas of chaos.

"He's good," Kenji said, his voice a low murmur. "Too good."

"But not perfect," Sarah replied, her voice a low whisper. She had found a flaw, a tiny crack in the digital armor of their unseen enemy. It was a ghost in the machine, a digital echo that had been left behind, a whisper in the cacophony of data.

They followed the thread, a digital breadcrumb that led them through a labyrinth of firewalls and encrypted networks. They were chasing a shadow, a digital phantom who was always one step ahead, always aware of their presence. It was a game of cat and mouse, a digital dance of death.

"He knows we're here," Kenji said, his voice a low growl. The digital phantom was toying with them, leaving them false trails, digital dead ends. It was a game, a challenge, a test of their skills.

"But he's also arrogant," Sarah replied, her voice a low whisper. "And arrogance is a weakness."

She had found another flaw, another crack in the armor. It was a subtle mistake, a digital slip of the tongue. But it was enough. It was a clue, a breadcrumb, a signpost that pointed them in the right direction.

They followed the new thread, a digital lifeline that led them to a name, a whisper in the digital wind. "The Serpent," Kenji said, his voice a low murmur. The name was a ghost, a legend, a myth in the underworld of arms dealers and mercenaries. He was a phantom, a man with no face, no past, no identity. He was the one who had supplied the nuclear device, the one who had orchestrated the attack.

"Find him," Marcus said, his voice a low command. He had been watching them work, a silent observer in their digital dance. He knew that The Serpent was the key, the one who could lead them to the heart of The Syndicate.

Kenji and Sarah redoubled their efforts, their fingers a blur on the keyboard as they chased the digital ghost of The Serpent. They were in his world now, a world of shadows and lies, a world where nothing was as it seemed. But they were not afraid. They were hunters. And they were closing in on their prey.

They found him in Geneva, a city of secrets and spies, a place where the world's power brokers met in the shadows. He was a ghost, a phantom, a man who did not exist. But he had made a mistake. He had left a digital footprint, a tiny echo of his presence. And it was enough.

"We've got him," Sarah said, her voice a low whisper. She had his location, a digital pin in the map of the world. He was in a private bank, a fortress of secrets and lies. He was meeting with someone, a ghost from the shadows, a player in the deadly game they were all a part of.

"Let's go," Marcus said, his voice a low command. The hunt was on. And the ghosts were coming for their prey.

The war against The Syndicate was fought on two fronts: the physical and the digital. While Marcus and his team prepared for the ground assault, Kenji and Sarah waged their own war in the virtual world, a battle of code and data that was as deadly as any firefight.

They worked in a room that was a symphony of screens and servers, a digital nerve center that was the heart of their operation. Their fingers were a blur on the keyboard, their eyes a reflection of the data that was their lifeblood. They were a team of digital hunters, a pair of ghosts who could navigate the darkest corners of the internet.

"The Syndicate's network is a fortress," Kenji explained, his voice a low murmur. "They're using a decentralized system, a web of ghost servers that are constantly shifting location. It's designed to be untraceable."

"But nothing is truly untraceable," Sarah added, a glint of determination in her eyes. "Every system has a weakness, a back door, a crack in the armor. We just have to find it."

They worked through the night, their minds a whirlwind of algorithms and code. They probed the edges of The Syndicate's network, looking for a way in, a thread they could pull to unravel the whole tapestry. It was a game of cat and mouse, a digital dance of death.

They found it in a series of encrypted communications, a pattern that was hidden in the noise. It was a ghost in the machine, a digital echo that had been left behind by a careless operative. They followed the thread, a digital lifeline that led them to the heart of The Syndicate's operations.

"We've got them," Sarah said, her voice a triumphant whisper. "We've found their command and control server. It's in Geneva, hidden in a private bank."

The digital battlefield had yielded its first victory. They had found a way in, a crack in the armor of the enemy. The hunt was on. And the ghosts were closing in.

# Chapter 7: The Geneva Connection

Geneva was a city of pristine beauty, a facade of order and civility that masked a world of secrets and lies. The private jet touched down on the tarmac, a sleek bird of prey in a city of swans. Marcus and his team disembarked, a group of ghosts in a city of phantoms. They were in enemy territory now, a world where the rules of engagement were as fluid as the waters of the lake that gave the city its name.

They moved through the city with the quiet efficiency of seasoned professionals, their movements a study in stealth and precision. They were a team of shadows, a group of ghosts who could walk through walls and disappear in the blink of an eye. They were in their element.

They set up a command center in a nondescript hotel room, a sterile space that was a world away from the luxury and opulence of the city outside. Kenji and Sarah were at their keyboards, their fingers a blur as they monitored the digital world, their eyes a reflection of the data that was their lifeblood. Javier was a whirlwind of motion, his hands a blur as he prepared his tools of the trade, a collection of explosives and gadgets that could turn a fortress into a pile of rubble. Anya was a silent observer, her gaze sharp, her instincts on high alert. She was the one who would see the threat before it materialized, the one who would sense the danger before it struck.

Marcus stood at the window, his gaze fixed on the city below. He was a hunter in a jungle of concrete and steel, a predator in a world of prey. He was waiting for the right moment, the right opportunity to strike.

"He's on the move," Kenji said, his voice a low murmur. The Serpent was leaving the bank, a ghost in a city of phantoms. He was in a black sedan, a sleek bird of prey that was moving through the city with a sense of purpose.

"Stay with him," Marcus said, his voice a low command. He was already in motion, his team a whirlwind of activity as they prepared to follow their prey.

They moved through the city like a pack of wolves, their movements a study in coordinated precision. They were a team of hunters, a group of ghosts who were closing in on their prey. They followed the black sedan through the winding streets of the city, their own vehicle a shadow in its wake.

The sedan stopped at a private airfield on the outskirts of the city, a place where the world's elite came and went in the shadows. The Serpent disembarked, a tall, elegant figure in a tailored suit. He was a man who exuded an aura of power and danger, a man who was used to being in control.

He was met by another man, a figure who was a ghost from Marcus's past, a man he had hoped he would never see again. Viktor, the arms dealer who had kidnapped Tori, the man who had been a part of the conspiracy that had nearly destroyed his life. He was a ghost from the shadows, a phantom from a past that would not stay buried.

"Viktor," Marcus said, his voice a low growl. The name was a curse, a bitter taste in his mouth. He had thought Viktor was dead, a casualty of the battle that had been the climax of their last encounter. But he was here, in the flesh, a ghost from the past who had returned to haunt him.

"He's not supposed to be here," Anya said, her voice a low whisper. She had been there, had been a part of the battle that had supposedly ended Viktor's reign of terror.

"Apparently, he's harder to kill than we thought," Marcus replied, his voice a low growl. He watched as Viktor and The Serpent embraced, a meeting of two devils in a city of angels. They were partners, two sides of the same coin, two players in the deadly game that was unfolding.

They boarded a private jet, a sleek bird of prey that was preparing to take flight. They were leaving, disappearing into the shadows, their destination a mystery.

"We can't let them get away," Javier said, his voice a low growl. He was already reaching for his tools of the trade, his eyes a reflection of the fire that was burning in his soul.

"We won't," Marcus said, his voice a low command. He was already in motion, his team a whirlwind of activity as they prepared to follow their prey. The hunt was on. And the ghosts were not about to let their prey escape.

Geneva was a city of quiet wealth and hidden secrets, a place where the world's elite came to hide their money and their sins. It was a city of banks and diplomats, a neutral ground where the rules of the outside world did not apply. It was the perfect hiding place for The Syndicate's financial operations.

Marcus and his team arrived in the city under the cover of darkness, a team of ghosts who were about to walk into the lion's den. They set up a command center in a nondescript apartment, a sterile space that was a world away from the opulent streets below.

Their target was a private bank, a discreet institution that catered to the world's wealthiest and most secretive clients. It was a fortress of security, a place that was designed to be impenetrable. But the ghosts were masters of their craft. They were a team of hunters who could not be denied.

Javier, with his expertise in explosives, identified a weakness in the building's security system. It was a back door, a vulnerability that had been overlooked by the bank's designers. It was a way in, a path that would allow them to bypass the main security and reach the heart of the operation.

Anya, with her skills in infiltration, would lead the way. She was a ghost in the shadows, a woman who could move through the world without a sound. She would be the first one in, the one who would clear the path for the rest of the team.

Marcus and Elena would be the muscle, the warriors who would deal with any resistance they encountered. They were a father and daughter who were a force to be reckoned with, a team of hunters who were about to deliver a devastating blow to the enemy.

The Geneva connection was a key node in The Syndicate's network, a vital organ that they could not afford to lose. If they could cut off their money, they could cripple their operations. They could force them to make a mistake.

The ghosts were ready. The hunt was about to enter a new phase. And the world was about to feel the wrath of Phoenix and his team.

# Chapter 8: The Trail to the Devil's Archipelago

The private jet was a silver bullet in the night sky, a ghost in the darkness that was carrying two of the world's most dangerous men to an unknown destination. But they were not alone. Marcus and his team were in hot pursuit, their own jet a shadow in the night, a bird of prey that was closing in on its quarry.

Kenji and Sarah were a whirlwind of activity in the back of the jet, their fingers a blur on the keyboard as they tracked the flight path of their target. They were in a digital dogfight, a high-stakes game of cat and mouse in the virtual world. The Serpent's people were good, a team of digital ghosts who were trying to shake their pursuers. But Kenji and Sarah were better. They were a team of digital hunters, a pair of ghosts who could not be shaken.

"They're heading east," Kenji said, his voice a low murmur. "Towards Southeast Asia."

"Any idea where?" Marcus asked, his voice a low command. He was standing over them, his gaze fixed on the screen, his mind a whirlwind of calculations and strategies.

"Not yet," Sarah replied, her voice a low whisper. "They're good. They're bouncing their signal off a series of satellites, making it almost impossible to track."

"Almost," Kenji said, a grin on his face. He had found a flaw, a tiny crack in their digital armor. It was a ghost in the machine, a digital echo that had been left behind. It was a clue, a breadcrumb, a signpost that pointed them in the right direction.

They followed the thread, a digital lifeline that led them to a name, a whisper in the digital wind. "The Devil's Archipelago," Kenji said, his voice a low murmur. The name was a legend, a myth in the underworld of mercenaries and arms dealers. It was a chain of volcanic islands in the South China Sea, a place that was not on any map, a place that did not officially exist. It was a pirate's haven, a fortress of secrets and lies, a place where the world's most dangerous men could disappear without a trace.

"That's where they're going," Marcus said, his voice a low growl. "That's their base of operations. That's the heart of The Syndicate."

He looked at his team, his family. He saw the fear in their eyes, the uncertainty. The Devil's Archipelago was a place of nightmares, a place from which no one had ever returned. But he also saw a resolve, a determination, a loyalty that was as strong as steel. They were in. All of them.

"So what's the plan?" Javier asked, his voice a low growl. He was already checking his equipment, his eyes a reflection of the fire that was burning in his soul.

"The plan is simple," Marcus said, his voice a low command. "We go in. We find them. And we burn their world to the ground."

He looked at them, his team, his family. He saw the ghosts of their past in their eyes, the shadows of the battles they had fought together. But he also saw a strength, a resilience, a loyalty that had not faded with time. They were ready. They were a team of ghosts, a group of hunters who were about to walk into the devil's den.

The jet changed course, a silver bullet in the night sky that was now heading towards the heart of the storm. The trail to the Devil's Archipelago was a one-way ticket to hell. But for Marcus and his team, it was a journey they had to take. It was a journey to the heart of darkness, a journey to the final battle that would decide the fate of the world.

The Geneva operation was a success, a surgical strike that sent a shockwave through The Syndicate's network. They had crippled their financial hub, had exposed their money laundering operations, had forced them to scramble to cover their tracks. The ghosts had drawn first blood. The hunt was on.

But the victory was a hollow one. The intelligence they had gathered in Geneva pointed to a larger, more terrifying truth. The Syndicate was not just a financial empire. It was a military one as well. They had an army, a private force of mercenaries and soldiers who were being trained for a war that was about to engulf the world.

The trail led them to a place that was known only in whispers, a name that was spoken in the hushed tones of spies and assassins: the Devil's Archipelago. It was a chain of islands in the South Pacific, a remote and lawless territory that was the perfect hiding place for a shadow army.

"It's a fortress," Kenji explained, his voice a low murmur as he displayed the satellite imagery on the screen. "The main island is a military compound, a training ground for their soldiers. It's surrounded by a fleet of patrol boats and a network of surveillance drones. Getting in will be like walking into a hornet's nest."

Marcus studied the images, his mind a whirlwind of tactical analysis. The Devil's Archipelago was a formidable target, a place that was designed to be impenetrable. But he had faced worse odds before. He had walked through the world's darkest corners and had emerged, scarred but unbroken.

"We don't have a choice," he said, his voice a low command. "If we don't take out their army, they'll use it to launch their next attack. We have to go in."

The trail to the Devil's Archipelago was a path into the heart of darkness. It was a mission that would test them to their limits, a battle that would determine the fate of the world. The ghosts were ready. The hunt was about to reach its climax.

# Chapter 9: Inside the Fortress

The Devil's Archipelago was a place of nightmares, a chain of volcanic islands that rose from the sea like the jagged teeth of some mythical beast. The air was thick with the smell of sulfur and salt, a toxic cocktail that was a fitting perfume for the devil's den. The main island was a fortress, a natural stronghold that had been augmented with the latest in military technology. It was a place that was designed to keep the world out, a place where the world's most dangerous men could hide from the prying eyes of the law.

Marcus and his team approached the island under the cover of darkness, their small inflatable boat a ghost on the water. They were a team of shadows, a group of hunters who were about to walk into the lion's den. They moved with the quiet efficiency of seasoned professionals, their movements a study in stealth and precision.

They landed on a secluded beach, a small strip of black sand that was hidden from the prying eyes of the island's security cameras. They moved into the jungle, a dense, tangled mess of vegetation that was a world away from the pristine beauty of Whidbey Island. The air was thick with the sounds of the jungle, a symphony of unseen creatures that was a fitting soundtrack for the heart of darkness.

They moved through the jungle like a pack of wolves, their movements a study in coordinated precision. They were a team of hunters, a group of ghosts who were closing in on their prey. They were heading for the main compound, a fortress of concrete and steel that was the heart of The Syndicate's operations.

They reached the perimeter of the compound, a high-tech fence that was a formidable barrier. But for Javier, it was just another puzzle to be solved. He was a master of his craft, a man who could turn a fortress into a pile of rubble with a few well-placed charges. He worked with the quiet efficiency of a surgeon, his hands a blur as he disabled the fence's security system. The fence was down. The ghosts were in.

They moved through the compound like a team of shadows, their movements a study in stealth and precision. They were in the heart of the beast now, a world of soldiers and mercenaries, a place where a single mistake could mean a swift and brutal death. But they were not afraid. They were hunters. And they were closing in on their prey.

They found the main building, a towering structure of concrete and steel that was the nerve center of the compound. It was a fortress within a fortress, a place where The Serpent and Viktor were hiding. They were in the throne room, a high-tech command center from which they were orchestrating their war on the world.

Marcus and his team moved through the building like a team of ghosts, their movements a study in coordinated precision. They were a team of hunters, a group of shadows who were about to come face to face with the devils they had been hunting.

They reached the throne room, a massive chamber that was a symphony of high-tech equipment and armed guards. The Serpent and Viktor were there, two devils on their thrones, their faces a portrait of arrogance and power. They were surrounded by their praetorian guard, a team of elite soldiers who were the best that money could buy.

"Welcome, Phoenix," The Serpent said, his voice a low, sibilant hiss. He had been expecting them. He had known they were coming. It was a trap.

"It's over, Serpent," Marcus said, his voice a low growl. He was standing in the doorway, his team a line of shadows behind him. They were outnumbered, outgunned. But they were not outmatched.

"Is it?" The Serpent replied, a cruel smile on his face. "I think it's just beginning."

The battle began, a whirlwind of violence and chaos. It was a dance of death, a symphony of destruction. Marcus and his team were a blur of motion, a team of ghosts who were fighting for their lives, for the fate of the world. They were outnumbered, but they were not outmatched. They were a team of warriors, a family of hunters who would not be denied.

The approach to the Devil's Archipelago was a journey into the unknown, a voyage across a sea that was as treacherous as the enemy they were about to face. They traveled in a small, unmarked boat, a ghost on the water, their movements a study in stealth and precision.

They landed on a secluded beach on the main island, a small strip of black sand that was hidden from the compound's surveillance. They moved into the jungle, a dense, tangled mess of vegetation that was both a shield and a prison. The air was thick with the smell of decay, a grim reminder of the death that awaited them.

They moved through the jungle like a pack of wolves, their movements a study in coordinated precision. They were a team of hunters, a group of ghosts who were closing in on their prey. They reached the perimeter of the compound, a high-tech fence that was designed to keep out the world.

Javier, with his expertise in explosives, found a way through. He disabled the sensors, cut through the wire, and created a breach that would allow them to enter the compound undetected. It was a masterful piece of work, a testament to his skill and his nerve.

They moved through the breach, a team of shadows in a city of soldiers. The compound was a hive of activity, a military base that was preparing for war. They saw soldiers training, weapons being loaded, vehicles being fueled. It was a terrifying sight, a glimpse of the army that The Syndicate was about to unleash on the world.

They moved through the compound with a grim determination, their hearts heavy with the weight of the mission. They were not just soldiers. They were ghosts, haunted by the memories of the battles they had fought, the comrades they had lost. But they were also warriors, a team of hunters who would not be denied.

They were inside the fortress. The heart of darkness was within their reach. And the final battle was about to begin.

# Chapter 10: The Heart of Darkness

The throne room was a maelstrom of violence, a whirlwind of bullets and blood. Marcus and his team were a force of nature, a team of ghosts who were cutting a swath of destruction through the ranks of The Serpent's guards. They were outnumbered, but they were not outmatched. They were a family of warriors, a team of hunters who were fighting with a desperation that was born of love and loyalty.

Marcus was a blur of motion, his movements a symphony of violence. He was a predator in his natural element, a man who had been forged in the crucible of a hundred battles. He moved through the room like a ghost, his hands a blur as he dispatched his enemies with a brutal efficiency.

Elena was at his side, a whirlwind of motion in her own right. She was her father's daughter, a warrior who had been born in the shadows. She moved with a grace and a precision that was both beautiful and terrifying, her movements a dance of death that was a mirror of her father's.

Javier was a whirlwind of destruction, his explosives a symphony of chaos. He was a master of his craft, a man who could turn a fortress into a pile of rubble with a few well-placed charges. He was a force of nature, a man who was a one-man army.

Anya was a silent predator, her movements a study in stealth and precision. She was a ghost in the shadows, a woman who could kill with a touch, a whisper, a glance. She was a phantom, a woman who was as deadly as she was beautiful.

Kenji and Sarah were the digital ghosts, their fingers a blur on the keyboard as they fought their own battle in the virtual world. They were a team of hunters, a pair of ghosts who were tearing down the digital walls of The Syndicate's empire.

Viktor was a ghost from the past, a man who had returned from the dead to haunt Marcus. He was a skilled fighter, a man who was a match for Marcus in every way. They met in the center of the room, two titans clashing in a battle that was a lifetime in the making. It was a dance of death, a symphony of violence that was a mirror of the chaos that was raging around them.

Marcus was driven by a cold fury, a rage that was born of the love he felt for his family, the loyalty he felt for his team. He was fighting for his life, for his family, for the world. He was fighting for the future, for a world where his daughter would not have to live in the shadows, a world where his wife would not have to fear the ghosts of his past.

He was Phoenix, the man who had walked through the world's darkest corners, the man who had stared into the heart of darkness and had not blinked. He was a warrior, a hunter, a ghost. And he would not be denied.

He defeated Viktor, the ghost from his past, in a brutal, hand-to-hand battle that left them both battered and bruised. He stood over him, his chest heaving, his body a canvas of pain. He had won. He had defeated the ghost from his past. But the battle was not over.

The Serpent was still there, a devil on his throne, a cruel smile on his face. He had been watching the battle, a spectator in his own coliseum. He was not a fighter. He was a puppeteer, a man who pulled the strings from the shadows. But he was not a coward. He had a final card to play.

He pressed a button on his console, a button that would unleash a new kind of hell on the world. He had a network of nuclear devices, a web of terror that was spread across the globe. He was a madman, a devil who was willing to burn the world to the ground.

"It's over, Phoenix," he said, his voice a low, sibilant hiss. "You may have won the battle. But I have already won the war."

But he had underestimated the ghosts. He had underestimated their loyalty, their skill, their determination. Kenji and Sarah had been one step ahead, had already found the kill switch, the digital key that could disarm the network of terror.

"Not today, Serpent," Sarah said, her voice a low whisper. She pressed a button on her own console, a button that sent a digital kill signal to the network of terror. The bombs were disarmed. The world was safe.

The Serpent's face was a mask of disbelief, of rage, of defeat. He had lost. He had been outplayed, outmaneuvered, outsmarted. He was a devil who had been cast out of his own hell.

He reached for a gun, a final act of defiance. But he was too slow. Marcus was faster. A single shot rang out, a final note in the symphony of destruction. The Serpent fell, a devil who had been slain by a ghost.

The battle was over. The heart of darkness had been silenced. The world was safe. But the war was not over. The Syndicate was a hydra, a beast with many heads. They had cut off one, but others would rise to take its place. The ghosts had won the battle. But the war was far from over.

# ACT II: INTO THE SHADOWS

The heart of the compound was a throne room, a grand chamber that was a monument to the ego of the man who ruled it. It was a place of opulence and terror, a space where The Serpent held court, where he dispensed justice and death with equal measure.

Marcus and his team fought their way to the throne room, a whirlwind of violence and chaos. The battle was a brutal, close-quarters affair, a dance of death in the corridors of the compound. They were outnumbered, but they were not outmatched. They were a team of warriors, a family of hunters who were fighting for the future of the world.

They reached the throne room, a grand chamber that was guarded by The Serpent's elite soldiers. The battle was fierce, a clash of two armies of ghosts. Marcus and Elena were a whirlwind of motion, a father and daughter who were a force to be reckoned with. Javier and Anya were a symphony of destruction, a pair of warriors who were wreaking havoc on the ranks of the enemy.

And in the center of it all, seated on a throne of black marble, was The Serpent himself. He was a man of indeterminate age, his face a mask of cold, calculating intelligence. He watched the battle with a detached amusement, a king observing the chaos of his court.

"Phoenix," he said, his voice a low, sibilant hiss. "I've been expecting you."

Marcus faced him, his chest heaving, his body a canvas of pain. "It's over, Serpent," he said, his voice a low growl. "Your empire is crumbling. Your army is gone. You've lost."

"Have I?" The Serpent replied, a cruel smile on his face. "You've won a battle, Phoenix. But the war is far from over. The world is a chaotic, messy place. It needs a firm hand, a guiding vision. It needs a serpent."

The final confrontation was at hand. The heart of darkness had been reached. And the fate of the world was hanging in the balance.

# Chapter 11: The Bangkok Connection

The victory at the Devil's Archipelago was a hollow one. They had cut off the head of the snake, but the body was still writhing, its venom still potent. The Syndicate was a hydra, a beast with many heads, and they had only just begun to fight.

The flight back from the heart of darkness was a somber affair. The adrenaline had faded, leaving behind a bone-deep weariness, a sense of profound loss. They had won the battle, but the war was far from over. The ghosts were tired, their bodies battered, their souls bruised.

They returned to Whidbey Island, to the sanctuary of Marcus's home, a place that seemed a world away from the violence and chaos they had just endured. But the peace was a fragile thing, a delicate bubble that had been shattered by the return of the shadows.

Tori was waiting for them, her expression a mixture of relief and fear. She ran into Marcus's arms, holding him tight, her tears a warm rain on his chest. "You're back," she whispered, her voice a soft melody. "You're all back."

He held her, his own heart a battlefield of conflicting emotions. He was home, but he was not whole. A part of him was still in the throne room, in the heart of darkness, a part of him that would never be the same.

They gathered in the war room, a room that had become the nerve center of their new reality. The mood was grim, the air thick with the unspoken understanding that their victory had been a temporary one. The Syndicate was still out there, a shadowy threat that was lurking in the darkness.

"We need to find the other heads of the hydra," Marcus said, his voice a low growl. "We need to dismantle their network, piece by piece."

Kenji and Sarah were already at work, their fingers a blur on the keyboard as they sifted through the mountain of data they had downloaded from The Serpent's servers. It was a digital treasure trove, a map of The Syndicate's empire, a web of connections that spanned the globe.

They found a thread, a digital breadcrumb that led them to Bangkok, a city of vibrant chaos and hidden secrets. It was a hub of The Syndicate's operations, a place where they laundered their money, recruited their soldiers, and planned their next move.

"There's a name," Sarah said, her voice a low whisper. "Chai, a Thai general who's on The Syndicate's payroll. He's their man in Bangkok, the one who facilitates their operations in Southeast Asia."

"Then he's our next target," Marcus said, his voice a low command. "We cut off their money, we cut off their power."

He looked at his team, his family. He saw the weariness in their eyes, the toll that the last battle had taken on them. But he also saw a resolve, a determination, a loyalty that had not been broken. They were ready. They were a team of ghosts, a group of hunters who were about to walk into the lion's den once more.

"Get some rest," he said, his voice a low rumble. "We leave for Bangkok in the morning."

The ghosts dispersed, each to their own corner of the house, each to their own private battle with the demons of their past. Marcus found Tori on the deck, her gaze fixed on the turbulent waters of the Sound. He walked towards her, his steps heavy, his heart a leaden weight in his chest.

"I'm sorry," he whispered, the words inadequate, a pale shadow of the apology he owed her.

"Don't be," she replied, her voice steady despite the tears that shimmered in her eyes. "Just... be careful."

He pulled her into his arms, holding her tight, the scent of her hair a familiar comfort in a world that had suddenly become alien and hostile. "Always," he promised, his voice a low growl. "I will always be careful."

He held her for a long time, the two of them a small island of love and hope in a world that was teetering on the brink of chaos. The Bangkok connection was a new thread in the web of The Syndicate's empire, a new battle in a war that was far from over. The ghosts were tired, but they were not broken. And they would not rest until the world was safe.

Bangkok was a city of contrasts, a place where ancient temples stood beside gleaming skyscrapers, where the sacred and the profane existed in an uneasy harmony. It was a city of secrets, a place where information was the most valuable currency, where the right whisper in the right ear could change the course of history.

Marcus and his team arrived in the city under the cover of darkness, a team of ghosts who were following a trail that had led them from the Devil's Archipelago to the heart of Southeast Asia. The intelligence they had gathered from The Serpent's compound had pointed to a new threat, a new node in The Syndicate's network that was operating in the shadows of the city.

They set up a command center in a nondescript hotel, a sterile space that was a world away from the vibrant chaos of the streets below. Kenji and

Sarah, the digital ghosts, were already at work, their fingers a blur on the keyboard, their eyes a reflection of the data that was their lifeblood.

"The Bangkok connection is a logistics hub," Kenji explained, his voice a low murmur. "It's where The Syndicate moves their weapons, their money, their people. It's the heart of their supply chain."

"If we can take it out," Sarah added, "we can cripple their operations. We can cut off their lifeline."

The target was a shipping company, a legitimate business that was a front for The Syndicate's illegal activities. It was a fortress of security, a place that was designed to be impenetrable. But the ghosts were masters of their craft. They were a team of hunters who could not be denied.

They spent days watching the target, learning its rhythms, its patterns, its weaknesses. They identified the key players, the guards, the schedules. They mapped out the building, the entrances, the exits, the blind spots. They were a team of hunters, and they were preparing for the kill.

The Bangkok connection was a vital organ in The Syndicate's body. If they could cut it out, they could weaken the enemy, could force them to make a mistake. The ghosts were ready. The hunt was about to enter a new phase.

# Chapter 12: Racing Against Time

Bangkok was a city of sensory overload, a vibrant tapestry of sights, sounds, and smells. It was a city of contrasts, a place where ancient temples stood in the shadow of gleaming skyscrapers, where the scent of incense mingled with the fumes of a thousand tuk-tuks. It was a city of secrets, a place where anything could be bought or sold, a place where a man's life was a cheap commodity.

Marcus and his team moved through the city like a team of ghosts, their movements a study in stealth and precision. They were in their element, a group of hunters in a jungle of concrete and steel. They set up a command center in a nondescript apartment in the heart of the city, a sterile space that was a world away from the vibrant chaos of the streets below.

Kenji and Sarah were at their keyboards, their fingers a blur as they monitored the digital world, their eyes a reflection of the data that was their lifeblood. They were tracking Chai, the corrupt general who was The Syndicate's man in Bangkok. He was a ghost, a man who moved in the shadows, a man who was careful to cover his tracks. But he was not careful enough.

They found him in a high-end brothel in the city's red-light district, a place where the city's elite came to indulge their darkest desires. He was meeting with a group of men, a collection of ghosts from the shadows, players in the deadly game they were all a part of.

"We've got him," Sarah said, her voice a low whisper. She had his location, a digital pin in the map of the city. He was vulnerable, exposed, a target that was ripe for the taking.

"Let's go," Marcus said, his voice a low command. He was already in motion, his team a whirlwind of activity as they prepared to move in for the kill.

They moved through the city like a pack of wolves, their movements a study in coordinated precision. They were a team of hunters, a group of ghosts who were closing in on their prey. They reached the brothel, a gaudy, neon-lit building that was a monument to the city's sins. They moved in, a team of shadows in a house of pleasure.

The battle was swift, brutal, and silent. They moved through the building like a team of ghosts, their movements a symphony of violence. They were a force of nature, a team of hunters who were not to be denied. They took down Chai's guards with a brutal efficiency, their movements a blur of motion in the dim light of the brothel.

They found Chai in a private room, a look of shock and fear on his face. He was a man who was used to being in control, a man who was not used to being the prey. He reached for a gun, a final act of defiance. But he was too slow. Marcus was faster. He disarmed him with a single, fluid motion, his hand a blur of motion.

"It's over, Chai," Marcus said, his voice a low growl. He was standing over him, his expression a mask of grim resolve.

"Who are you?" Chai asked, his voice a trembling whisper.

"We're the ghosts you should have been afraid of," Marcus replied, his voice a low command. "Now, you're going to tell us everything you know about The Syndicate."

Chai was a broken man, his arrogance shattered, his power gone. He sang like a canary, his words a torrent of information, a map of The Syndicate's operations in Southeast Asia. He told them about the money laundering, the drug trafficking, the arms dealing. He told them about the network of corrupt officials, the web of spies and informants, the army of soldiers and mercenaries. He told them everything.

But he also told them something else, something that sent a jolt of ice through Marcus's veins. The Syndicate was planning another attack, a new act of terror that would make the attack on the *USS Roosevelt* look like a child's game. They were planning to detonate a dirty bomb in Washington D.C., a city that was the heart of the free world.

"When?" Marcus asked, his voice a low growl.

"Soon," Chai replied, his voice a trembling whisper. "Very soon."

They were racing against time, a desperate sprint to prevent a catastrophe that would plunge the world into a new era of darkness. The ghosts had won another battle, had cut off another head of the hydra. But the war was far from over. And the clock was ticking.

The assault on the Bangkok logistics hub was a race against time, a desperate gamble that could tip the balance of the war. The intelligence they had gathered pointed to a new threat, a shipment of weapons that was about to leave the city, a cargo of death that could be used to launch a devastating attack on the West.

They moved in the dead of night, a team of shadows in a city of lights. The streets were a maze of neon and noise, a chaotic symphony that was the perfect cover for their operation. They moved through the crowds like ghosts, their movements a study in stealth and precision.

They reached the shipping company, a fortress of concrete and steel that was surrounded by a wall of security. Javier, with his expertise in explosives, created a diversion, a controlled blast that drew the guards away from the main entrance. It was a masterful piece of work, a testament to his skill and his nerve.

Anya led the way, a ghost in the shadows, her movements a blur of lethal grace. She took out the remaining guards with a silent efficiency, her body a weapon that was as deadly as any gun. She was a predator, a hunter, a woman who was in her element.

Marcus and Elena followed, a father and daughter who were a force to be reckoned with. They moved through the building like a whirlwind, their movements a symphony of violence and precision. They were a team of warriors, a family of hunters who were fighting for the future of the world.

They found the shipment in a warehouse, a collection of crates that were filled with weapons of mass destruction. It was a terrifying sight, a glimpse of the carnage that The Syndicate was planning to unleash on the world. They had to stop it. They had to destroy it.

Javier went to work, his hands a blur of motion as he rigged the crates with explosives. It was a delicate operation, a dance of death that required a steady hand and a cool head. He was a master of his craft, a man who could turn destruction into an art form.

They were racing against time, a desperate gamble that could save the world. The clock was ticking. The hunt was reaching its climax.

# Chapter 13: The Journey to the Devil's Archipelago

The news of the impending attack on Washington D.C. was a gut punch, a jolt of ice that sent a chill through the hearts of Marcus and his team. They were racing against time, a desperate sprint to prevent a catastrophe that would make the attack on the *USS Roosevelt* look like a minor skirmish. The stakes had been raised. The game had become a matter of life and death for millions of innocent people.

They left Bangkok in a hurry, a team of ghosts who were disappearing into the night. They were heading back to the Devil's Archipelago, to the heart of darkness, to the place where The Syndicate had been born. They knew that the key to stopping the attack was there, hidden in the ashes of The Serpent's empire.

Kenji and Sarah were a whirlwind of activity on the jet, their fingers a blur on the keyboard as they sifted through the mountain of data they had downloaded from Chai's servers. It was a digital treasure trove, a map of The Syndicate's operations, a web of connections that spanned the globe. But it was also a labyrinth, a maze of false trails and dead ends, a digital puzzle that was designed to confuse and mislead.

They were looking for a needle in a haystack, a digital breadcrumb that would lead them to the location of the dirty bomb. They were chasing a ghost, a digital phantom who was always one step ahead, always aware of their presence. It was a game of cat and mouse, a digital dance of death.

"He's good," Kenji said, his voice a low murmur. "He's very good."

"But he's not perfect," Sarah replied, her voice a low whisper. She had found a flaw, a tiny crack in the digital armor of their unseen enemy. It was a ghost in the machine, a digital echo that had been left behind, a whisper in the cacophony of data.

They followed the thread, a digital lifeline that led them to a name, a whisper in the digital wind. "Kain," Kenji said, his voice a low murmur. The name was a ghost from Marcus's past, a man he had thought was long dead, a man who had been his partner, his friend, his brother in arms. Kain had been a member of Phoenix's original team, a man who had walked through the world's darkest corners with him. But he had been corrupted, had been turned by the darkness, had become a monster.

"Kain is alive?" Marcus asked, his voice a low growl. The name was a curse, a bitter taste in his mouth. He had been the one to report Kain's death, had been the one to close the book on his friend's betrayal. But it had all been a lie.

"He's more than alive, Marcus," Sarah said, her voice a low whisper. "He's the one who designed the dirty bomb. He's the one who's planning the attack on Washington."

The news was a betrayal that cut deeper than any knife. Kain had been his friend, his brother. And now, he was his enemy, a monster who was threatening to burn the world to the ground.

"We have to stop him," Marcus said, his voice a low command. "We have to stop him before it's too late."

They were heading back to the Devil's Archipelago, to the heart of darkness, to the place where Kain was hiding. The journey was a somber affair, a silent vigil for a friendship that had been lost, a brotherhood that had been broken. The ghosts were tired, their bodies battered, their souls bruised. But they were not broken. And they would not rest until the world was safe.

The journey back to the Devil's Archipelago was a voyage into the heart of darkness, a return to the place where the final battle would be fought. The intelligence they had gathered in Bangkok had revealed a terrifying truth: The Serpent was still alive, still in control, still planning his war on the world.

They traveled in a military transport, a ghost plane that was invisible to radar, a shadow in the sky. The mood was grim, the air thick with the unspoken understanding that they were about to walk into the lion's den. They had been to the Devil's Archipelago before. They knew what awaited them.

Marcus sat in the cargo hold, his eyes fixed on the darkness outside the window. He was a man at war, a warrior who was about to face his greatest challenge. The Serpent was a formidable enemy, a man who had built an empire of shadows, a man who had the resources and the ruthlessness to bring the world to its knees.

Elena sat beside him, her hand finding his in the darkness. She was his daughter, a warrior in her own right, a woman who had earned the right to stand beside him. She was his strength, his anchor, his reason for fighting.

"We're going to win this," she said, her voice a fierce whisper. "We're going to stop them."

He looked at her, his heart swelling with a pride that was almost painful. She was his legacy, a warrior who would carry on the fight long after he was gone. She was the future, a beacon of hope in a world that was filled with shadows.

"I know," he replied, his voice a low rumble. "We're a family. And nothing can stop us."

The journey to the Devil's Archipelago was a path into the unknown, a voyage into the heart of darkness. But they were not afraid. They were a team of ghosts, a family of hunters. And they were ready for whatever came next.

# Chapter 14: Breaching the Fortress

The Devil's Archipelago was a different place the second time around. The fortress was in a state of chaos, the once-impenetrable stronghold now a scene of devastation. The battle with The Serpent had left its mark, a scar on the face of the island that would never fade. The ghosts had returned to the scene of their victory, but the taste of triumph was a bitter one.

They approached the island under the cover of darkness, their small inflatable boat a ghost on the water. They were a team of shadows, a group of hunters who were walking back into the lion's den. But this time, they were not just hunters. They were avengers.

They landed on the same secluded beach, a small strip of black sand that was now littered with the debris of battle. They moved into the jungle, a dense, tangled mess of vegetation that was now a graveyard of fallen soldiers. The air was thick with the smell of death, a grim reminder of the price of victory.

They moved through the jungle like a pack of wolves, their movements a study in coordinated precision. They were a team of hunters, a group of ghosts who were closing in on their prey. They were heading for the main compound, a fortress of concrete and steel that was now a tomb.

They reached the perimeter of the compound, a high-tech fence that was now a twisted wreck of metal and wire. They moved through the breach, a team of shadows in a city of the dead. The compound was a ghost town, a silent testament to the battle that had been fought there. The bodies of The Serpent's soldiers were everywhere, a grim tableau of death and destruction.

They moved through the compound with a sense of grim determination, their hearts heavy with the weight of the lives that had been lost. They were not just soldiers. They were ghosts, haunted by the memories of the battles they had fought, the comrades they had lost.

They found the main building, a towering structure of concrete and steel that was now a hollow shell. They moved through the building like a team of ghosts, their movements a study in coordinated precision. They were looking for Kain, the ghost from their past, the man who was threatening to burn the world to the ground.

They found him in the throne room, the same room where they had defeated The Serpent. He was standing in the center of the room, a solitary figure in a sea of destruction. He was a ghost from the past, a man who had been consumed by the darkness. He was a monster.

"Hello, Marcus," he said, his voice a low, sibilant hiss. He had been expecting them. He had known they were coming. It was a trap.

"It's over, Kain," Marcus said, his voice a low growl. He was standing in the doorway, his team a line of shadows behind him. They were outnumbered, outgunned. But they were not outmatched.

"Is it?" Kain replied, a cruel smile on his face. "I think it's just beginning."

He was not alone. A team of elite soldiers emerged from the shadows, a group of ghosts who were as deadly as they were silent. They were Kain's personal guard, a team of killers who were loyal to him and him alone.

The battle began, a whirlwind of violence and chaos. It was a dance of death, a symphony of destruction. Marcus and his team were a blur of motion, a team of ghosts who were fighting for their lives, for the fate of the world. They were outnumbered, but they were not outmatched. They were a team of warriors, a family of hunters who would not be denied.

The approach to the Devil's Archipelago was a masterpiece of tactical planning, a coordinated assault that was designed to overwhelm the enemy's defenses. They came from the sea and the sky, a two-pronged attack that would catch The Serpent's forces off guard.

The sea team, led by Marcus and Elena, approached the main island in a fleet of small, fast boats. They were ghosts on the water, their movements a study in stealth and precision. They landed on a secluded beach, a small strip of black sand that was hidden from the compound's surveillance.

The air team, led by Javier and Anya, dropped from the sky in a HALO jump, a high-altitude, low-opening descent that was designed to avoid detection. They landed in the jungle, a dense, tangled mess of vegetation that was both a shield and a prison.

They converged on the compound, a pincer movement that was designed to crush the enemy between two forces. The battle was fierce, a clash of two armies of ghosts. The Serpent's forces were well-trained, well-armed, and well-prepared. But they were not prepared for the fury of the Sterling team.

Marcus and Elena were a whirlwind of motion, a father and daughter who were a force to be reckoned with. They fought their way through the compound, their movements a symphony of violence and precision. They were a team of warriors, a family of hunters who were fighting for the future of the world.

Javier and Anya were a symphony of destruction, a pair of warriors who were wreaking havoc on the ranks of the enemy. Javier's explosions were a thunderous counterpoint to Anya's silent kills, a deadly duet that was tearing the compound apart.

The fortress was breached. The heart of darkness was within their reach. And the final battle was about to begin.

# Chapter 15: The Throne Room

The throne room was a crucible of violence, a whirlwind of bullets and blood. The battle was a brutal, close-quarters affair, a dance of death in a room that had already seen too much of it. Marcus and his team were a force of nature, a team of ghosts who were fighting with a desperation that was born of betrayal and a burning desire for justice.

Marcus and Kain were a whirlwind of motion in the center of the room, two titans clashing in a battle that was a lifetime in the making. It was a brutal, personal affair, a fight between two brothers who had become mortal enemies. They were a mirror of each other, two sides of the same coin, two men who had been forged in the same fire. But one had been consumed by the darkness, while the other had found his way back to the light.

Their movements were a symphony of violence, a dance of death that was both beautiful and terrifying. They were two masters of their craft, two men who knew each other's every move, every thought, every weakness. It was a battle of wills, a test of strength, a fight to the death.

Elena was a whirlwind of motion at her father's side, a warrior who was fighting with a ferocity that was born of love and a burning desire to protect her family. She was a ghost in the shadows, a woman who was as deadly as she was beautiful. She moved with a grace and a precision that was a mirror of her father's, her movements a dance of death that was a testament to the blood that flowed in her veins.

Javier was a force of nature, a one-man army who was wreaking havoc on the ranks of Kain's soldiers. He was a master of his craft, a man who could turn a fortress into a pile of rubble with a few well-placed charges. He was a whirlwind of destruction, a man who was a symphony of chaos.

Anya was a silent predator, a ghost in the shadows who was dispatching her enemies with a brutal efficiency. She was a phantom, a woman who could kill with a touch, a whisper, a glance. She was a master of her craft, a woman who was as deadly as she was beautiful.

Kenji and Sarah were the digital ghosts, their fingers a blur on the keyboard as they fought their own battle in the virtual world. They were a team of hunters, a pair of ghosts who were tearing down the digital walls of Kain's empire. They were looking for the dirty bomb, the weapon of terror that was the key to Kain's plan. They were racing against time, a desperate sprint to prevent a catastrophe that would plunge the world into a new era of darkness.

They found it, a digital breadcrumb that led them to a location in Washington D.C., a place where the bomb was hidden, waiting to be detonated. They had the location. They had the key. But they were running out of time.

"We've got it, Marcus," Sarah said, her voice a low whisper. "But we're running out of time. The bomb is set to go off in less than an hour."

The news was a jolt of ice that sent a chill through Marcus's heart. He was still locked in a deadly dance with Kain, a battle that seemed to have no end. He had to finish it. He had to finish it now.

He found a new strength, a new resolve, a new fury. He was fighting for his family, for his team, for the world. He was fighting for the future, for a world where his daughter would not have to live in the shadows, a world where his wife would not have to fear the ghosts of his past.

He was Phoenix, the man who had walked through the world's darkest corners, the man who had stared into the heart of darkness and had not blinked. He was a warrior, a hunter, a ghost. And he would not be denied.

He defeated Kain, the ghost from his past, in a brutal, final battle that left them both battered and bruised. He stood over him, his chest heaving, his body a canvas of pain. He had won. He had defeated the ghost from his past. But the battle was not over. The clock was still ticking.

The throne room was a monument to The Serpent's ego, a grand chamber that was filled with the spoils of his conquests. It was a place of opulence and terror, a space where he held court, where he dispensed justice and death with equal measure.

Marcus and his team fought their way to the throne room, a whirlwind of violence and chaos. The battle was a brutal, close-quarters affair, a dance of death in the corridors of the compound. They were outnumbered, but they were not outmatched. They were a team of warriors, a family of hunters who were fighting for the future of the world.

They reached the throne room, a grand chamber that was guarded by The Serpent's elite soldiers. The battle was fierce, a clash of two armies of ghosts. Marcus and Elena were a whirlwind of motion, a father and daughter who were a force to be reckoned with. Javier and Anya were a symphony of destruction, a pair of warriors who were wreaking havoc on the ranks of the enemy.

And in the center of it all, seated on a throne of black marble, was The Serpent himself. He was a man of indeterminate age, his face a mask of cold, calculating intelligence. He watched the battle with a detached amusement, a king observing the chaos of his court.

"Phoenix," he said, his voice a low, sibilant hiss. "You've come a long way to die."

Marcus faced him, his chest heaving, his body a canvas of pain. "I didn't come to die, Serpent," he said, his voice a low growl. "I came to end this."

The final confrontation was at hand. The throne room was a battlefield, a place where the fate of the world would be decided. And Marcus Sterling, the man who had been Phoenix, was ready to deliver the final blow.

# Chapter 16: The Fall of The Serpent

With Kain defeated, the throne room fell into a sudden, eerie silence. The remaining members of Kain's guard, seeing their leader fall, lost their will to fight. They dropped their weapons, their faces a mixture of fear and disbelief. The battle was over. The ghosts had won.

But there was no time for celebration. The clock was ticking, a relentless countdown to a catastrophe that would dwarf anything the world had ever seen. The dirty bomb in Washington D.C. was a sword of Damocles hanging over the head of the free world, a weapon of terror that had to be stopped.

"We're out of time," Marcus said, his voice a low growl. He was standing over Kain, his chest heaving, his body a canvas of pain. He looked at his former friend, his brother in arms, a man who had been consumed by the darkness. He saw a flicker of the man he had once known in Kain's eyes, a glimmer of regret, of remorse. But it was too late. The darkness had won.

"You can't stop it, Marcus," Kain whispered, his voice a hoarse rasp. "It's already in motion. The world will burn."

"Not today," Marcus replied, his voice a low command. He turned to his team, his family. "Let's go. We've got a bomb to catch."

They left the throne room, a team of ghosts who were disappearing into the night. They were leaving the Devil's Archipelago behind, a place of nightmares that would forever be a part of their story. They were heading for Washington D.C., to the heart of the storm, to the final battle that would decide the fate of the world.

The journey was a race against time, a desperate sprint across the globe. Kenji and Sarah were a whirlwind of activity on the jet, their fingers a blur on the keyboard as they guided the team on the ground in Washington. They had the location of the bomb, a digital pin in the map of the city. But it was a moving target, a ghost in the machine that was always one step ahead.

They were in a digital dogfight with Kain's people, a team of digital ghosts who were trying to protect their master's final legacy. But Kenji and Sarah were better. They were a team of digital hunters, a pair of ghosts who could not be shaken.

They found the bomb in a van, a nondescript vehicle that was moving through the streets of the city, a wolf in sheep's clothing. It was heading for the Capitol Building, the heart of American democracy, a symbol of the freedom that Kain had come to despise.

"We've got it," Sarah said, her voice a low whisper. "But we're running out of time. The bomb is set to go off in less than ten minutes."

The news was a jolt of ice that sent a chill through Marcus's heart. They were on the other side of the world, a team of ghosts who were helpless to stop the coming storm. But they were not alone. They had a team on the ground, a group of loyal soldiers who were ready to lay down their lives for the cause.

"Talk them through it, Sarah," Marcus said, his voice a low command. "You're their eyes and ears. You're their only hope."

Sarah's voice was a calm, steady presence in the chaos, a beacon of hope in a world that was teetering on the brink of darkness. She guided the team on the ground, her words a symphony of precision and control. She was a master of her craft, a woman who could see the patterns in the chaos, the order in the madness.

They found the van, a ghost in the city's traffic. They cornered it, a team of hunters who were closing in on their prey. The driver was a desperate man, a soldier who was willing to die for a cause he did not understand. He made a run for it, a final act of defiance. But he was no match for the team on the ground. They took him down, a ghost who had been vanquished by the light.

Javier was on the scene, a master of his craft who was now faced with the most difficult puzzle of his life. The bomb was a complex device, a symphony of wires and circuits that was designed to kill. He had to disarm it. He had to do it now.

He worked with a calm, steady hand, his movements a study in precision and control. He was a surgeon, a master of his craft who was performing a delicate operation on a patient that was about to explode. The clock was ticking, a relentless countdown to a catastrophe that would change the world forever.

He did it. With seconds to spare, he cut the final wire, a single, decisive act that saved the world. The bomb was disarmed. The threat was over. The world was safe.

The final battle with The Serpent was not a physical one, but a battle of wills, a clash of ideologies. Marcus, the warrior who had found his way back to the light, and The Serpent, the visionary who had been consumed by the darkness. It was a battle for the soul of the world.

The Serpent was a true believer, a fanatic who was convinced that he was saving the world by burning it down. He spoke of a new world order, a world where the chaos of democracy and freedom would be replaced by the order of a single, guiding hand. He was a man who could not be reasoned with, a man who had to be stopped.

"You think you're a hero, Phoenix," The Serpent said, his voice a low, mocking hiss. "But you're just a pawn, a tool of a system that is corrupt and broken. I'm offering the world a new beginning, a chance to start over."

"You're offering the world a dictatorship," Marcus replied, his voice a cold edge. "A world where one man decides who lives and who dies. That's not a new beginning. That's the end of everything."

The battle was joined, a clash of two warriors who were fighting for the future of the world. The Serpent was a formidable opponent, a man who had been trained in the same dark arts as Marcus. But Marcus had something The Serpent did not: a family, a team, a reason to fight that was stronger than any ideology.

In the end, it was not violence that won the day, but truth. Kenji and Sarah, the digital ghosts, had not only dismantled The Serpent's network; they had also gathered the evidence, the proof of his crimes, the blueprint of his plan for a new world order. They broadcast it to the world, a digital truth bomb that exposed The Serpent for what he was: a terrorist, a madman, a would-be dictator.

The Serpent was defeated, his empire in ruins, his dream of a new world order shattered. He was a broken man, a ghost who had been exposed to the light. The fall of The Serpent was a victory for the world, a triumph of light over darkness.

# Chapter 17: The Race to Washington

The disarming of the dirty bomb was a victory, a moment of triumph in a war that had been filled with so much loss. But the celebration was a muted one, a somber affair that was overshadowed by the knowledge that the war was not over. The Syndicate was a hydra, a beast with many heads, and they had only just begun to fight.

The flight to Washington D.C. was a journey of reflection, a time for the ghosts to lick their wounds and prepare for the next battle. They had won a major victory, had saved the world from a catastrophe that would have plunged it into a new era of darkness. But the cost had been high. They had lost friends, had shed blood, had stared into the heart of darkness and had been changed by what they had seen.

Marcus was a man in turmoil, his heart a battlefield of conflicting emotions. He had defeated his friend, his brother, a man he had once loved. He had saved the world, but he had lost a part of himself in the process. The ghosts of his past were whispering in his ear, their voices a constant reminder of the man he had been, the things he had done.

He found solace in the presence of his family, in the love of his wife, the strength of his daughter. They were his anchor in the storm, his reason to fight, his hope for a better future. He looked at them, his family, his world, and he knew that he would do whatever it took to protect them, to keep them safe from the shadows that were still lurking in the darkness.

They arrived in Washington D.C., a city that was a symbol of the freedom they had fought so hard to protect. The city was on high alert, a fortress of security in a world that was still reeling from the threat of The Syndicate. The ghosts were met by Colonel Jackson, the man who had pulled them back into the world of shadows. He was a man who was used to being in control, a man who was not used to being grateful. But there was a look of respect in his eyes, a silent acknowledgment of the debt that the world owed to the ghosts.

"You did good, Phoenix," he said, his voice a low rumble. "You did real good."

"It's not over, Jackson," Marcus replied, his voice a low growl. "The Syndicate is still out there. They're wounded, but they're not dead."

"I know," Jackson said, his voice grim. "But we've got them on the run. We're rounding up their people, dismantling their network, piece by piece. The world is a safer place because of you."

He led them to a secure facility, a place where they could rest, debrief, and prepare for the next battle. The ghosts were tired, their bodies battered, their souls bruised. But they were not broken. And they would not rest until the world was safe.

They spent the next few days in a whirlwind of debriefings and planning sessions, their minds a whirlwind of strategies and tactics. They were a team of hunters, a group of ghosts who were preparing for the final battle. They were a family of warriors, a team of hunters who would not be denied.

The fall of The Serpent was not the end of the war, but the beginning of a new phase. The intelligence they had gathered from his compound revealed a terrifying truth: a final attack was already in motion, a strike on the heart of American power that could not be stopped.

The target was Washington D.C., the capital of the free world. The Syndicate had planted a dirty bomb in the city, a weapon of mass destruction that was designed to kill thousands and spread terror across the globe. The clock was ticking, and the ghosts were the only ones who could stop it.

They raced to Washington, a team of warriors who were fighting against time. The city was a maze of streets and monuments, a place where the fate of the world was about to be decided. They had to find the bomb. They had to stop the attack. They had to save the world.

Kenji and Sarah, the digital ghosts, were their eyes and ears, guiding them through the city, tracking the signal of the bomb. They were a lifeline, a beacon of hope in a world that was on the brink of chaos.

Marcus and Elena led the ground team, a father and daughter who were a force to be reckoned with. They moved through the city like ghosts, their movements a study in stealth and precision. They were a team of hunters, and they were closing in on their prey.

Javier and Anya were the backup, a pair of warriors who were ready to provide support at a moment's notice. They were a symphony of destruction, a deadly duet that was ready to be unleashed.

The race to Washington was a desperate gamble, a final battle that would determine the fate of the world. The clock was ticking. The hunt was reaching its climax. And the ghosts were ready.

# Chapter 18: Victory in Washington

The days that followed were a blur of activity, a whirlwind of debriefings, planning sessions, and intelligence gathering. The ghosts were a well-oiled machine, a team of professionals who were working around the clock to dismantle the remnants of The Syndicate's empire. They were a force of nature, a team of hunters who were closing in on their prey.

Kenji and Sarah were the digital ghosts, their fingers a blur on the keyboard as they sifted through the mountain of data they had downloaded from The Serpent's and Kain's servers. They were a team of hunters, a pair of ghosts who were tearing down the digital walls of The Syndicate's empire. They were finding the other heads of the hydra, the other players in the deadly game that had almost brought the world to its knees.

They found them in the shadows, in the dark corners of the world where they had been hiding. They were a collection of ghosts, a group of men and women who had sold their souls for power and money. They were the ones who had pulled the strings, the ones who had orchestrated the chaos, the ones who had almost burned the world to the ground.

Marcus and his team moved with a swift and brutal efficiency, a team of ghosts who were delivering justice to the enemies of the free world. They were a force of nature, a team of hunters who were not to be denied. They took down the remaining heads of the hydra, one by one, a symphony of violence that was a testament to their skill, their courage, their loyalty.

The world watched in stunned silence as the truth about The Syndicate was revealed, a story of corruption, betrayal, and a lust for power that had reached the highest levels of government and finance. The world was in a state of shock, a state of disbelief. But it was also in a state of gratitude. The world owed a debt to the ghosts, a debt that could never be repaid.

The victory was a sweet one, a moment of triumph in a war that had been filled with so much loss. The ghosts had won. They had saved the world. They had stared into the heart of darkness and had emerged victorious.

They gathered in a secure room in the heart of Washington D.C., a team of warriors who had been to hell and back. They were a family, a band of brothers and sisters who had been forged in the crucible of battle. They had shed blood together, had faced death together, had saved the world together.

"It's over," Marcus said, his voice a low rumble. He looked at his team, his family. He saw the weariness in their eyes, the toll that the war had taken on them. But he also saw a sense of pride, a sense of accomplishment, a sense of peace. They had done it. They had won.

"So what now, boss?" Javier asked, his grin a flash of white in the dim light of the room.

"Now," Marcus said, a smile on his face, "we go home."

The bomb was hidden in a nondescript building in the heart of the city, a place that was designed to blend in with its surroundings. It was a ticking time bomb, a weapon of mass destruction that was about to unleash a wave of death and terror on the capital of the free world.

Marcus and his team moved in, a team of ghosts who were about to deliver the final blow. The building was guarded by The Syndicate's remaining forces, a desperate band of soldiers who were fighting for a lost cause. The battle was fierce, a clash of two armies of ghosts.

Marcus and Elena were a whirlwind of motion, a father and daughter who were a force to be reckoned with. They fought their way through the building, their movements a symphony of violence and precision. They were a team of warriors, a family of hunters who were fighting for the future of the world.

They found the bomb in the basement, a crude but deadly device that was designed to spread radioactive material across the city. Javier went to work, his hands a blur of motion as he defused the bomb. It was a delicate operation, a dance of death that required a steady hand and a cool head.

The clock was ticking, the seconds counting down to oblivion. But Javier was a master of his craft, a man who could turn destruction into an art form. He defused the bomb with seconds to spare, a final act of heroism that saved the city, that saved the world.

Victory in Washington was a triumph of light over darkness, a testament to the courage and the skill of the Sterling team. The war was over. The ghosts had won. And the world was safe, at least for now.

# Chapter 19: The Aftermath

The journey back to Whidbey Island was a journey of peace, a journey of hope, a journey to a future that was no longer shrouded in darkness. The ghosts were going home, their mission accomplished, their war won. They were a family of warriors, a team of hunters who had earned their rest.

They arrived on the island to a hero's welcome, a quiet celebration that was a world away from the chaos and violence they had left behind. Tori was there, her face a portrait of love and relief. She ran into Marcus's arms, her tears a warm rain on his chest. "You're home," she whispered, her voice a soft melody. "You're finally home."

He held her, his own heart a symphony of emotions. He was home, and he was whole. The ghosts of his past had been vanquished, the shadows had been banished. He was free.

The days that followed were a time of healing, a time of reflection, a time of peace. The ghosts were a family, a band of brothers and sisters who had found a home, a sanctuary, a place where they could finally be themselves. They were no longer ghosts. They were a family.

Javier found a new purpose in teaching, his skills with explosives now used to train a new generation of soldiers. Anya returned to Tel Aviv, her skills now used to protect the innocent, to fight for justice. Kenji and Sarah started their own cybersecurity firm, their skills now used to protect the world from the digital ghosts who were still lurking in the shadows.

Marcus and Elena found a new purpose in their family, in the love that bound them together. They were a father and a daughter who had been forged in the crucible of battle, a bond that was as strong as steel. They were a family, a team, a force to be reckoned with.

They spent their days in the quiet serenity of Whidbey Island, their lives a symphony of peace and love. The shadows were gone, the ghosts were silent. The war was over.

But the world was a different place, a world that had been changed by the war with The Syndicate. The threat of nuclear terrorism was no longer a distant possibility. It was a real and present danger, a threat that had to be met with a new kind of vigilance, a new kind of courage.

The world needed heroes, a new generation of warriors who could walk in the shadows without being consumed by the darkness. The world needed a new kind of ghost, a new kind of hunter, a new kind of warrior.

And Marcus Sterling, the man who had been Phoenix, the man who had stared into the heart of darkness and had emerged victorious, knew that his work was not yet done. The war was over, but the battle for the future had just begun.

The aftermath of the war was a time of reckoning, a period of reflection on the battles that had been fought and the sacrifices that had been made. The Syndicate was in ruins, its leaders dead or in custody, its network dismantled. The world was a safer place, at least for now.

Marcus and his team returned to Whidbey Island, a team of weary warriors who were finally, truly, going home. The house on the bluff was a sanctuary, a place of peace and healing. It was a place where they could shed the weight of the war, where they could remember who they were, where they could find their way back to the light.

The world celebrated the victory, a triumph of light over darkness. The story of the Sterling team, the ghosts who had saved the world, was a sensation. They were heroes, a symbol of hope in a world that was still filled with shadows.

But for Marcus, the victory was a bittersweet one. He had seen too much, had done too much, had lost too much. The war had changed him, had scarred him in ways that would never fully heal. He was a warrior, a ghost, a man who had walked through the world's darkest corners. And he knew that the shadows would always be a part of him.

He stood on the deck of his home, watching the sun set over the Puget Sound. Tori was beside him, her hand in his, her presence a warmth that cut through the chill of the evening. Elena was on the beach below, her laughter a melody that was a balm to his soul.

"It's over," Tori said, her voice a soft whisper. "We can finally have peace."

"For now," Marcus replied, his voice a low rumble. "But the world is a dangerous place, Tori. There will always be new threats, new shadows, new battles to fight."

She looked at him, her eyes a reflection of the love they shared. "Then we'll face them together," she said, her voice a fierce vow. "As a family."

The aftermath of the war was a time of healing, a time of hope. The ghosts had won, had saved the world. And now, they had a chance to build a new future, a future that was defined not by their past, but by their love.

# Chapter 20: The Family Heals

The healing was a slow process, a journey of a thousand small steps. The ghosts were a family of warriors, a team of hunters who had been to hell and back. They had seen the darkness, had stared into the abyss, had been changed by what they had seen. The scars remained, both seen and unseen, a map of their journey through the heart of darkness.

Marcus was a man at peace, a warrior who had found his way back to the light. The ghosts of his past were silent, their whispers a distant echo in the chambers of his memory. He was a husband, a father, a man who had found his purpose in the love of his family.

He spent his days with Tori, their love a symphony of quiet moments, a dance of two souls who had been forged in the crucible of a shared past. They were a team, a partnership, a love story that was a testament to the power of hope, the resilience of the human spirit.

He spent his days with Elena, his daughter, his legacy. They were a father and a daughter who were learning to be a family, a team, a force to be reckoned with. They sparred in the gym, their movements a dance of violence that was a mirror of their shared past. They walked on the beach, their conversations a symphony of shared memories, a bridge across the chasm of their separate pasts. They were healing, together.

Elena was a young woman who was finding her way back to the light. The shadows of her past were still there, a constant reminder of the trauma she had endured. But they were no longer a prison. They were a part of her story, a map of her journey to this moment of peace, of hope, of love.

She was a warrior, a hunter, a woman who had been forged in the crucible of battle. But she was also a daughter, a friend, a woman who was learning to love, to trust, to hope.

The family was healing, together. They were a small island of love and hope in a world that was still reeling from the war with The Syndicate. The world was a different place, a world that had been changed by the threat of nuclear terrorism. The world needed heroes, a new generation of warriors who could walk in the shadows without being consumed by the darkness.

And Marcus Sterling, the man who had been Phoenix, the man who had stared into the heart of darkness and had emerged victorious, knew that his work was not yet done. The war was over, but the battle for the future had just begun. And he and his family, his team, his ghosts, would be ready.

# ACT III: THE HUNT

The weeks following the war were a time of quiet decompression. The adrenaline of the hunt faded, replaced by a deep, bone-weary exhaustion. The ghosts, no longer at war, had to learn to be at peace again. It was a transition that was as challenging as any battle they had fought.

Javier and Anya stayed for a while, their presence a comforting reminder of the family they had forged in the crucible of combat. The boisterous energy of Javier and the quiet intensity of Anya filled the house, a lively counterpoint to the island's tranquility. They were a part of the Sterling family now, bound by a loyalty that transcended blood.

There were long evenings spent around the fire pit, the flames dancing against the backdrop of the star-filled sky. They shared stories, not of war and violence, but of their lives before the shadows, of the people they had been, the dreams they had held. It was a form of therapy, a way of reclaiming the parts of themselves that had been lost in the darkness.

Elena, in particular, seemed to blossom in the peace. She was a young woman who was finally getting to know her father, the man behind the legend. She was seeing the cracks in the armor, the humanity beneath the warrior's façade. And she was loving him all the more for it.

Tori was the quiet center of these gatherings, her presence a source of warmth and stability. She was the one who had brought them all together, the one who had created this space of healing. She was the heart of their unconventional family.

The family was healing, slowly but surely. The scars of the war would never fully fade, but they were a part of their story, a map of their journey to this moment of quiet serenity. The ghosts had found their way back to the light. And they were ready for whatever came next.

# Chapter 21: Building a New Life

Time, they say, heals all wounds. But some wounds run so deep they become a part of the landscape of a person's soul, a geography of scars that tells a story of survival. For Marcus, Tori, and Elena, the years following the takedown of The Syndicate were a time of quiet rebuilding, a conscious effort to construct a new life on the foundations of a past that was riddled with the ghosts of violence and betrayal.

Whidbey Island became their sanctuary, a fortress of tranquility against the turbulent memories that still washed ashore with the tide. The house, once a war room and a command center, slowly transformed back into a home. The scent of cordite was replaced by the aroma of Tori's baking, the sharp crack of gunfire by the crackle of a log fire in the hearth. The maps of global conflict were taken down, replaced by Elena's artwork, vibrant splashes of color that were a testament to a spirit that refused to be broken.

Marcus found a semblance of peace in the rhythm of a civilian life he had never known. He took up woodworking, his hands, once instruments of death, now creating objects of beauty. He carved intricate figures from driftwood, his focus absolute, the repetitive motion a form of meditation that quieted the lingering whispers of Phoenix. He was a man learning to be still, to find solace not in the adrenaline of the fight, but in the quiet satisfaction of creation.

Elena, too, was on a journey of rediscovery. The warrior was still there, a coiled spring of lethal potential just beneath the surface, but she was also a young woman exploring the contours of a life that wasn't defined by survival. She enrolled in online university courses, her sharp mind devouring subjects from international relations to art history. She found a passion for photography, her eye capturing the rugged beauty of the island with the same precision she had once used to line up a target. Her camera became her new weapon, a tool to capture light instead of extinguishing it.

Tori was the anchor, the heart of their fragile new world. She nurtured their healing with a fierce and gentle love, creating a space where they could be vulnerable, where they could shed the armor they had worn for so long. She returned to her real estate business, her success a testament to her own strength and resilience. She was the bridge between their past and their future, a woman who had walked through the fire with them and had emerged not unscathed, but stronger.

But the peace was a fragile construct, a beautiful but thin veneer over the unquiet past. There were nights when Marcus would wake up in a cold sweat, the echoes of the throne room ringing in his ears. There were days when Elena's gaze would turn distant, her mind replaying the horrors she had endured. The shadows were patient. They lingered at the edges of their new life, a constant reminder that the world they had left behind was never truly far away.

They had built a new life, a good life. But they were still ghosts, in a way. Ghosts of a war that was over, but whose battles were still being fought in the quiet chambers of their hearts. They were a family forged in fire, bound by a love that was as fierce as it was tender. And they knew, with a certainty that was both a comfort and a quiet dread, that their story was not yet over.

The decision to build a new life was not a sudden one, but a gradual realization that had been growing in the quiet moments between the battles. Marcus, Tori, and Elena had been through hell together, had faced the darkness and had emerged, scarred but unbroken. They had earned the right to a new beginning, a chance to build something that was not defined by violence and destruction.

The house on Whidbey Island was transformed from a fortress into a home. The war room was converted into a study, a place where Marcus could read and reflect. The gym was softened with the addition of a yoga studio, a space where Tori could find her center. The guest rooms were filled with the laughter of friends and family, a constant reminder of the bonds they had forged.

Elena, in particular, seemed to thrive in the new environment. She enrolled in a local college, pursuing a degree in psychology. She wanted to understand the human mind, the forces that drove people to darkness and the paths that led them back to the light. She was a warrior who was learning to be a healer, a woman who was finding her own way.

Marcus found a new purpose in mentoring young veterans, men and women who had returned from war with the same scars he carried. He understood their pain, their struggles, their need to find a new identity. He was a guide, a counselor, a man who was using his experience to help others find their way back to the light.

Tori was the anchor, the heart of the family, the woman who kept them all grounded. She continued her work in real estate, but her focus shifted to helping veterans find homes, to building communities that supported those who had served. She was a force for good, a woman who was changing the world, one family at a time.

Building a new life was a journey, a process that required patience and perseverance. But the Sterling family was up to the challenge. They were a team, a family, a force for good. And they were ready for whatever came next.

# Chapter 22: The Bonds of Family

The process of healing was not a straight line, but a winding path with unexpected turns and hidden valleys. For the Sterling family, it was a journey they walked together, their bond the compass that guided them through the lingering shadows. The shared trauma had forged a connection between them that was deeper than blood, a silent understanding that needed no words.

Marcus and Elena's relationship, born in the crucible of violence, blossomed in the quiet of their island sanctuary. The gym, once a place of brutal training, became a space of connection. Their sparring sessions were less about combat and more about communication, a physical dialogue where they learned to read each other's movements, to anticipate each other's thoughts. It was a dance of trust, a way of speaking a language that went beyond words.

"You're telegraphing your right hook," Marcus would say, his voice a low rumble as he easily sidestepped her attack.

"And you're getting slow in your old age," she would retort, a playful glint in her eye as she feinted left and landed a soft jab to his ribs.

These moments were more than just training; they were a form of therapy. They were rebuilding a relationship that had been stolen from them, finding the father and daughter they might have been in a different, kinder world. They found common ground in their shared warrior spirit, but also in the quiet moments – walking the dogs on the beach, a comfortable silence between them, or working together in the garden, their hands in the earth, a symbol of their new, grounded life.

Elena and Tori's bond also deepened, a friendship growing between the woman who had been her captive and the woman who was now her stepmother. They found a shared language in art, spending hours in Elena's makeshift studio, Tori watching in awe as Elena transformed her pain into powerful images on canvas. Tori, in turn, shared her world with Elena, taking her to open houses, teaching her the art of the deal, showing her a life where success was measured not in body counts, but in happy clients and closed sales.

"You have a good eye for potential," Tori said one afternoon, as they stood in a dilapidated beachfront property. "You see the bones of a place, what it could be."

Elena looked at the crumbling walls, the salt-stained windows, and for the first time, she saw not decay, but possibility. It was a metaphor for her own life, a life that was being rebuilt from the ruins of her past.

Marcus and Tori's love, the bedrock of their family, was the force that held them all together. Theirs was a love that had been tested by fire and had emerged stronger, more resilient. They had learned to navigate the minefield of Marcus's past, to communicate their fears and their needs with a raw honesty. Their nights were no longer filled with nightmares, but with the quiet intimacy of two people who had found their safe harbor in each other's arms.

They were a family, a unique and unconventional one, but a family nonetheless. They were three individuals who had been broken in their own ways, but who were now healing, together. They were learning to be a family, to build a future, to believe in the possibility of a life that was not defined by the shadows. The bonds of family were their greatest strength, the shield that would protect them when the shadows inevitably returned.

The bonds of family were the strongest force in the Sterling household, a web of love and loyalty that held them together through the darkest of times. They were a family that had been forged in the crucible of

91

combat, a team of warriors who had become something more: a family.

The relationship between Marcus and Elena was a complex one, a bond that was still being defined. They were father and daughter, but they were also warriors, comrades who had fought side by side. They were learning to navigate the complexities of their relationship, to find the balance between the roles they played.

There were moments of tension, of misunderstanding, of the friction that comes from two strong personalities learning to coexist. But there were also moments of profound connection, of shared laughter and quiet understanding. They were a father and daughter who were learning to love each other, to trust each other, to be a family.

Tori was the bridge, the mediator, the woman who helped them navigate the complexities of their relationship. She was a mother to Elena, a wife to Marcus, a woman who was the heart of the family. She was the one who smoothed the rough edges, who healed the wounds, who brought them together.

The bonds of family were not always easy, but they were always worth it. They were the foundation on which the Sterling household was built, the strength that would carry them through whatever challenges lay ahead. They were a family, a team, a force for good. And nothing could break them apart.

# Chapter 23: The Shadows Return

Peace is a precious and often fleeting commodity for those who have lived in the world of shadows. For two years, the Sterling family had cultivated a life of quiet normalcy, a fragile peace that they guarded with a fierce protectiveness. But the past has a long reach, and the world of espionage is a small one. The shadows returned not with a bang, but with a whisper, a digital ghost that slipped through the cracks of their carefully constructed new life.

It started with a series of anomalies, digital breadcrumbs that only someone with Kenji's skills would notice. A string of untraceable donations to shell corporations, a spike in encrypted communications from blacklisted satellite networks, a pattern of movement of high-value assets that suggested something was being built, something big.

Kenji, now running a successful cybersecurity firm with Sarah, had kept a weather eye on the digital horizon, a silent guardian watching for the storms he knew were always gathering. He brought his concerns to Marcus, not as a former comrade, but as a friend.

"It's probably nothing," Kenji said, his voice a low murmur over the encrypted line. "But it feels... familiar. The architecture of the network, the way they're moving money. It has the signature of a state-level actor, but there's no state attached to it. It's a ghost organization."

The word 'ghost' was a trigger, a key that unlocked a door Marcus had tried so hard to keep closed. He felt a familiar chill, the cold premonition of a coming storm. He had hoped he was done, that Phoenix could finally rest. But the world had a way of pulling him back in.

He tried to dismiss it, to convince himself that it was just Kenji being paranoid. But the seed of unease had been planted. He started paying attention, his old instincts, long dormant, slowly waking up. He noticed the black sedan that was parked a little too long down the road, the faint static on their phone line, the drone that flew a little too close to their property.

Then came the package. A simple, unmarked manila envelope left on their doorstep. Inside, there was no note, no threat, just a single, high-resolution photograph. It was a picture of Elena, taken from a distance, as she was sketching on the beach. She was unaware, vulnerable. It was a message, a clear and chilling statement: *We see you. We can reach you.*

The peace was shattered. The sanctuary had been breached. The shadows had returned.

Marcus's transformation was instantaneous. The quiet woodworker disappeared, and Phoenix was back, his eyes cold and hard, his mind a whirlwind of tactical analysis. He gathered Tori and Elena in the gym, the one room in the house that was still a fortress, a secure space that was swept for bugs daily.

"They've found us," he said, his voice a low growl as he showed them the photograph. "I don't know who 'they' are yet, but they're sending a message."

Tori's face went pale, her hand flying to her mouth. But there was no fear in Elena's eyes. Only a cold, hard fury. The warrior, the survivor, was back.

"So what do we do?" she asked, her voice steady, her gaze locked on her father's.

"We do what we do best," Marcus replied, his voice a low command. "We hunt."

The shadows had returned, and with them, the ghosts. The Sterling family, the team of warriors who had been forged in the crucible of battle, was about to go to war once more.

The peace was not destined to last. The world was a dangerous place, and the shadows had a way of returning, of reminding them that the war was never truly over. The first sign of trouble came in the form of a news report, a story that sent a chill down Marcus's spine.

A series of coordinated attacks had struck targets across Europe, a wave of violence that bore the hallmarks of a new threat. The attacks were sophisticated, well-planned, and utterly ruthless. They were the work of a professional organization, a group that had the resources and the expertise to strike at the heart of the Western world.

Marcus watched the news with a growing sense of dread. He recognized the patterns, the tactics, the signature of an enemy he had thought was defeated. The Syndicate was gone, but something new had risen in its place, a new threat that was even more dangerous.

"It's not over," he said, his voice a low rumble. "It's never over."

Tori was beside him, her hand finding his. "What do we do?" she asked, her voice a mixture of fear and determination.

"We do what we always do," he replied, his eyes fixed on the screen. "We fight."

The shadows had returned, a new threat that was emerging from the darkness. The ghosts were being called back to the hunt, a team of warriors who were needed once more. The war was not over. It was just beginning.

# Chapter 24: The Investigation Begins

The photograph was a declaration of war, a violation that turned their sanctuary into a potential battlefield. The immediate response was a lockdown. The house on Whidbey Island, once a symbol of their peaceful new life, reverted to its true nature: a fortress. The security systems were upgraded, the perimeter reinforced, and a new set of protocols was established. The ghosts were back on a war footing.

But defense was only half the battle. The real work began in the gym, their ad-hoc command center. The photograph was the first clue, a tangible piece of evidence in a puzzle that was still mostly shadows. Marcus, his Phoenix persona now fully in control, began the painstaking process of deconstructing the threat.

"They're professionals," he said, his voice a low murmur as he examined the photograph under a magnifying glass. "The shot was taken from over 800 meters. Long lens, high-powered camera. They knew the blind spots in our surveillance. They've been watching us for a while."

Elena, her own analytical skills sharpened by years of survival, pointed to a small detail in the corner of the photo. "The metadata has been scrubbed, obviously. But look at the light. The angle of the sun. This was taken three days ago, in the late afternoon."

They were a team, a father and daughter who spoke the same language of threat assessment and tactical analysis. While they worked the physical evidence, Kenji and Sarah launched a full-scale assault on the digital front. The ghost organization that Kenji had detected was their prime suspect. They began to map its network, to follow the money, to peel back the layers of its digital camouflage.

"They're using a decentralized network, a series of ghost servers that are constantly shifting location," Kenji reported, his voice a low hum over the secure line. "It's a sophisticated setup, designed to be untraceable. But they made a mistake."

He explained that the satellite that had transmitted the photograph had a unique digital handshake, a signature that he had been able to isolate. It was a long shot, but if they could track the satellite's path, they might be able to find the location of the person who had sent the image.

Meanwhile, Marcus reached out to his own network of contacts, the ghosts of his past who were still scattered across the globe. He sent a single, encrypted message: "Phoenix is calling. A new shadow has fallen. Information is currency."

The response was slow at first, a trickle of whispers from the dark corners of the intelligence world. But then, a name emerged, a whisper that sent a chill down Marcus's spine: "The Chimera."

It was a name he had heard before, a ghost story that was told in the hushed tones of spies and assassins. The Chimera was a legend, a mythical organization that was said to be a black-ops-for-hire group, a team of deniable assets who would do the dirty work that governments couldn't afford to be associated with. They were said to be the best, the most ruthless, the most untraceable.

"If it's The Chimera," Marcus said, his voice grim, "then we're in a whole new level of trouble. These aren't just criminals. They're a private army of ghosts, with the skills and resources of a state intelligence agency."

The investigation had yielded its first terrifying results. They had a name for their enemy, a glimpse of the scale of the threat they were facing. The Chimera. A beast of myth and legend, a monster with many heads. And it had set its sights on the Sterling family.

The investigation into the new threat was a descent into a world of shadows and secrets, a journey that would take them to the darkest corners of the globe. Marcus reached out to his network, the contacts he had cultivated over a lifetime of service, the ghosts who still walked in the shadows.

The intelligence they gathered painted a picture of a new enemy, a group that called itself The Chimera. It was a hydra-headed organization, a coalition of criminal syndicates, rogue intelligence agents, and terrorist cells that had come together under a single, unifying vision. They were the children of The Syndicate, a new generation of darkness that had learned from the mistakes of their predecessors.

"They're smarter than The Syndicate," Kenji explained, his voice a low murmur. "They're decentralized, compartmentalized. They don't have a single leader, a single point of failure. They're a network, a web of cells that can operate independently."

"That makes them harder to track," Sarah added. "But it also makes them harder to control. They're a coalition of competing interests, a group that is held together by a shared enemy: us."

Marcus studied the intelligence, his mind a whirlwind of analysis. The Chimera was a formidable enemy, a threat that would require all of their skills, all of their resources, all of their courage. But he had faced worse odds before. He had walked through the world's darkest corners and had emerged, scarred but unbroken.

"We need to find their leadership," he said, his voice a low command. "We need to cut off the head of the hydra."

The investigation was just beginning, a journey into the heart of darkness. The ghosts were on the hunt once more. And they would not rest until the threat was neutralized.

# Chapter 25: The Gathering Storm

The name 'Chimera' changed the equation. This was no longer a simple matter of a criminal organization seeking revenge. This was a professional hit, orchestrated by a group that was as skilled and as ruthless as they were. The photograph of Elena was not just a threat; it was a calling card, a statement of capability. The storm was gathering, and the Sterling family was in its eye.

The first priority was to get Elena off the island. She was the target, the vulnerability they were trying to exploit. But Elena, a warrior in her own right, refused to run.

"No," she said, her voice firm, her gaze unwavering. "I'm not a damsel in distress. I'm a part of this team. I'm not leaving."

Marcus saw the same fire in her eyes that he saw in the mirror every morning. She was his daughter, and she was a fighter. He knew he couldn't protect her by hiding her away. He could only protect her by fighting alongside her.

"Alright," he said, a reluctant pride in his voice. "But you follow my orders, no questions asked. We do this my way."

She nodded, a silent agreement passing between them. The family was united. They would face this storm together.

The investigation intensified, a race against time to understand the enemy before they could strike again. Kenji and Sarah worked tirelessly, their digital hunt for The Chimera yielding more and more disturbing information. They were a global organization, with cells in every major city, a network of spies and assassins that was as vast as it was invisible.

They discovered that The Chimera had a leader, a shadowy figure who was known only as "The Architect." He was a ghost, a man with no name, no face, no past. He was the one who pulled the strings, the one who designed the operations, the one who had sent the photograph.

Marcus's network of contacts began to bear fruit. A former colleague from his Phoenix days, a man who was now a high-ranking official in the CIA, sent him a cryptic message: "The Chimera is real. They're a deniable-ops group that was created by a rogue faction within the agency. They were supposed to be a weapon. But the weapon has turned on its masters."

The pieces of the puzzle were starting to come together, forming a picture that was more terrifying than they could have imagined. The Chimera was not just a group of mercenaries. They were a product of the same world that had created Phoenix, a dark reflection of the very forces that Marcus had once served.

Then came the second message from The Chimera. This time, it was not a photograph. It was a direct communication, a single line of text that appeared on Marcus's encrypted laptop: "We know who you are, Phoenix. And we're coming for you."

The message was a direct challenge, a gauntlet thrown down. The storm had arrived. The hunt was on. And the Sterling family was no longer the prey. They were the hunters.

The gathering storm was a time of preparation, a period of intense activity as the Sterling team readied themselves for the battle ahead. The house on Whidbey Island was once again transformed into a command center, a hive of activity where the ghosts were planning their next move.

Javier and Anya returned, their presence a comforting reminder of the family they had forged in the crucible of combat. They were a part of the Sterling team, bound by a loyalty that transcended borders and nationalities. They were ready to fight, ready to die, ready to do whatever it took to stop The Chimera.

Kenji and Sarah, the digital ghosts, were already at work, their fingers a blur on the keyboard, their eyes a reflection of the data that was their lifeblood. They were the eyes and ears of the operation, the ones who would guide the team through the digital battlefield.

Elena was a full member of the team now, a warrior who had earned her place at the table. She was her father's daughter, a woman who was as lethal as she was intelligent. She was ready to fight, ready to prove herself, ready to be a part of the family legacy.

The gathering storm was a time of tension and anticipation, a period of waiting for the battle to begin. The ghosts were ready. The hunt was about to resume. And the world was about to feel the wrath of the Sterling team.

# Chapter 26: The New Threat

The direct communication from The Architect was a paradigm shift. The enemy was no longer a faceless entity; it had a voice, an arrogant, taunting voice that was confident in its own power. The game had changed. This was personal.

"They're not just trying to kill us," Marcus said, his voice a low growl as he stared at the message on his laptop. "They're trying to dismantle us, to break us. This is a psychological game as much as it is a physical one."

He knew this kind of enemy. He had been this kind of enemy. The Chimera was a mirror of his own past, a dark reflection of the world he had tried so hard to leave behind. They were not just soldiers; they were strategists, manipulators, masters of the art of war.

Kenji and Sarah, digging deeper into the digital entrails of The Chimera, uncovered the true nature of the new threat. This was not about revenge for the takedown of The Syndicate. This was about something much bigger.

"They're not just a black-ops-for-hire group," Sarah reported, her voice grim. "They're building something. A private intelligence network, a global surveillance system that will be more powerful than anything the CIA or the NSA has. They're using their operations to fund it, to steal the technology, to recruit the talent. They're building a shadow government."

The new threat was not just a physical one; it was an existential one. The Chimera was not just trying to kill them; they were trying to replace the world order with one of their own making, a world where they were the ones who pulled the strings, the ones who controlled the flow of information, the ones who held the power.

And Marcus, the legendary Phoenix, was a threat to their plans. He was a ghost from the old world, a man with the skills and the knowledge to expose them, to stop them. He was a loose end that had to be tied up.

"So they're not just hunting us," Elena said, her voice a low whisper. "They're hunting what we represent. The old guard. The ones who still believe in things like loyalty and justice."

"Exactly," Marcus replied, his voice a low command. "And that's why we have to stop them. This isn't just about us anymore. This is about the future."

The new threat was clear. The Chimera was not just a group of assassins; they were a nascent superpower, a shadow government in the making. And the Sterling family was standing in their way.

They knew they couldn't fight this war alone. They were a formidable team, but they were outnumbered and out-resourced. They needed allies. They needed to assemble a new team, a new group of ghosts who were willing to walk into the shadows and fight for a world that was on the brink of a new kind of darkness.

The new threat was unlike anything they had faced before. The Chimera was not a single organization, but a network of cells, a web of competing interests that were united by a shared goal: the destruction of the Western world. They were a hydra, a many-headed beast that could not be killed by cutting off a single head.

The intelligence they gathered revealed a terrifying truth: The Chimera was planning a series of coordinated attacks, a campaign of terror that would destabilize the global order and plunge the world into chaos. They had the resources, the expertise, and the ruthlessness to make it happen.

"They're not just terrorists," Marcus explained, his voice a low rumble. "They're a new kind of enemy. They're a coalition of the world's most dangerous players, a group that has learned from the mistakes of The Syndicate. They're smarter, more decentralized, more dangerous."

The team studied the intelligence, their faces a mask of grim determination. They knew what they were up against, the scale of the threat they were facing. But they were not afraid. They were a team of ghosts, a family of hunters. And they were ready for whatever came next.

"We need to find their leadership," Elena said, her voice a fierce determination. "We need to cut off the head of the hydra."

"There is no single head," Kenji replied, his voice a low murmur. "But there is a brain, a central intelligence that is coordinating their operations. If we can find it, we can take them down."

The new threat was a formidable one, a challenge that would test them to their limits. But the ghosts were ready. The hunt was on. And they would not rest until the threat was neutralized.

# Chapter 27: Assembling the New Team

The decision to build a new team was a pragmatic one, born of the understanding that The Chimera was too big, too powerful, too widespread to be fought by a family of three, no matter how skilled. They needed a team of specialists, a group of ghosts who could match The Chimera's skills and who were willing to operate in the shadows, outside the lines of conventional warfare.

Marcus, Tori, and Elena gathered in the war room, the list of potential recruits a testament to a life lived on the front lines of the secret world. The names were a collection of ghosts, a who's who of the world's most dangerous and most effective operatives. Some were old friends, comrades from Marcus's Phoenix days. Others were former enemies, men and women who had earned his respect in the crucible of battle.

First on the list was Javier, the explosives expert who had been a key part of the team that had taken down The Syndicate. He was a man who could turn a fortress into a pile of rubble with a few well-placed charges, a man whose loyalty was as unshakable as his nerve. He was teaching at a military academy, but Marcus knew that the call to action would be one he couldn't resist.

Next was Anya, the former Mossad agent who had been a part of the same team. She was a silent predator, a master of infiltration and close-quarters combat, a woman who could move through the world like a ghost. She had returned to Tel Aviv, but her skills were too valuable to be left on the sidelines.

Then there was Kenji and Sarah, the digital ghosts who were already a part of the team. They were the best in the world at what they did, a pair of hackers who could tear down the digital walls of any fortress. They were the eyes and ears of the operation, the ones who would guide the team through the digital battlefield.

But they needed more. They needed someone on the inside, someone with access to the kind of intelligence that only a government agency could provide. Marcus made a call to Colonel Jackson, the man who had pulled him back into the world of shadows. It was a risky move, a step back into a world he had tried so hard to leave behind. But he had no choice.

"I need your help, Jackson," Marcus said, his voice a low growl. "I need your resources, your intelligence, your blessing to operate in the shadows."

Jackson was a pragmatist, a man who understood that the world was not a black and white place. He knew that The Chimera was a threat that had to be stopped, a threat that the government couldn't fight in the open. He agreed to help, to provide the support they needed, to give them the deniability they required.

With Jackson's support, the new team was assembled. Javier and Anya arrived on Whidbey Island, their faces a mixture of grim determination and a quiet excitement. They were warriors, hunters, ghosts who were ready to go to war once more.

The new team was a family of warriors, a band of brothers and sisters who had been forged in the crucible of battle. They were a team of specialists, a group of ghosts who were about to walk into the heart of darkness. The hunt was on. And the new team was ready.

The battle against The Chimera would require a new kind of team, a coalition of specialists who could match the enemy's decentralized structure. Marcus reached out to his network, the contacts he had cultivated over a lifetime of service, the ghosts who still walked in the shadows.

They came from around the world, a collection of warriors who had answered the call. There was Viktor, a former Spetsnaz operative who had defected to the West, a man whose skills in infiltration were legendary. There was Mei, a former Chinese intelligence agent who had been burned by her own government, a woman whose expertise in cyber warfare was unmatched. There was Omar, a former Jordanian special forces soldier who had lost his family to terrorism, a man whose hatred of extremism was a fire that could not be extinguished.

They gathered at the house on Whidbey Island, a team of ghosts who were about to walk into the lion's den. The mood was grim, the air thick with the unspoken understanding that some of them might not return. But they were warriors, a team of hunters who had chosen this life. They were ready.

"We're a new kind of team," Marcus said, his voice a low command. "We're not bound by borders, by nationalities, by politics. We're bound by a shared purpose: to stop The Chimera, to protect the innocent, to fight for a world that is worth living in."

The new team was assembled, a coalition of specialists who were ready to take on the most dangerous enemy they had ever faced. The hunt was about to begin. And the ghosts were ready.

# Chapter 28: The Hunt Begins

The assembly of the new team transformed the house on Whidbey Island back into a full-fledged command center. The quiet sanctuary was now a hive of activity, a nerve center for a global hunt. The ghosts were back together, a family of warriors who were preparing for a war that would be fought in the shadows, a war for the future of the world.

The first step was to go on the offensive. They could no longer afford to be the prey; they had to become the hunters. They had to take the fight to The Chimera, to disrupt their operations, to dismantle their network, to force them out of the shadows.

Kenji and Sarah, with the full resources of their cybersecurity firm and the backing of Colonel Jackson's intelligence, launched a multi-pronged assault on The Chimera's digital infrastructure. They were a team of digital ghosts, a pair of hunters who were tearing down the walls of The Architect's digital fortress. They were looking for a weakness, a crack in the armor, a way to get inside.

They found it in a series of encrypted communications that were being routed through a server in Geneva. It was a financial hub, a place where The Chimera was laundering their money, funding their operations, building their shadow government. It was a key node in their network, a vital organ that they could not afford to lose.

"If we can cut off their money," Marcus said, his voice a low command, "we can cripple their operations. We can force them to make a mistake."

The plan was a classic Phoenix operation: a surgical strike, a swift and silent assault that would leave the enemy reeling. Marcus, Elena, Javier, and Anya would go to Geneva, a team of ghosts who would walk into the lion's den. Kenji and Sarah would be their eyes and ears, their digital guides through the labyrinth of the city's financial district.

They arrived in Geneva, a city of quiet wealth and hidden secrets. They moved through the city like a team of ghosts, their movements a study in coordinated precision. They set up a command center in a sterile hotel room, a temporary home for a team of hunters who were about to go to war.

They identified their target: a private bank, a discreet institution that was a front for The Chimera's money laundering operations. It was a fortress of security, a place that was designed to be impenetrable. But the ghosts were masters of their craft. They were a team of hunters who could not be denied.

Javier, the master of explosives, found a way in. He identified a weakness in the building's ventilation system, a back door that would allow them to bypass the main security. Anya, the master of infiltration, would lead the way, a ghost in the shadows who could move through the building without a sound.

Marcus and Elena would be the muscle, the warriors who would deal with any resistance they encountered. They were a father and daughter who were a force to be reckoned with, a team of hunters who were about to deliver a devastating blow to the enemy.

The hunt had begun. The ghosts were on the move. And the world was about to feel the wrath of Phoenix and his team.

The hunt for The Chimera was a global operation, a coordinated assault that would take them to the darkest corners of the world. They followed the trail of intelligence, a digital breadcrumb that led them from one cell to the next, from one target to the next.

They struck in Berlin, dismantling a cell that was planning an attack on the German parliament. They struck in Cairo, taking out a group of arms dealers who were supplying The Chimera with weapons. They struck in Tokyo, exposing a network of hackers who were planning to bring down the Japanese financial system.

Each victory was a blow to The Chimera, a wound that weakened the beast. But the hydra was resilient, a many-headed monster that could regenerate, that could adapt, that could survive. For every cell they destroyed, another seemed to rise in its place.

"We're making progress," Kenji said, his voice a low murmur. "But we're not winning. We're playing whack-a-mole, taking out cells as they pop up. We need to find the brain, the central intelligence that is coordinating their operations."

Marcus nodded, his expression a mask of grim determination. "Then we dig deeper," he said, his voice a low command. "We follow the money, the communications, the patterns. We find the brain. And we cut it out."

The hunt was a marathon, not a sprint, a war of attrition that would test their endurance, their resolve, their will to fight. But the ghosts were relentless, a team of hunters who would not be denied. The hunt was on. And they would not rest until the threat was neutralized.

# Chapter 29: The Mediterranean Assault

The Geneva operation was a success, a surgical strike that sent a shockwave through The Chimera's network. They had crippled their financial hub, had exposed their money laundering operations, had forced them to scramble to cover their tracks. The ghosts had drawn first blood. The hunt was on.

But The Chimera was a wounded beast, and a wounded beast is a dangerous one. They retaliated, not with a direct assault, but with a move that was designed to be both a distraction and a demonstration of their power. They launched an attack on a series of oil tankers in the Mediterranean, a coordinated assault that was designed to create chaos in the global markets, to show the world that they could strike anywhere, anytime.

Colonel Jackson's intelligence confirmed that the attacks were the work of The Chimera. They were using a team of highly trained mercenaries, a group of ghosts who were operating from a hidden base in the Mediterranean. It was a bold move, a public display of their power, a challenge to the world.

"They're trying to draw us out," Marcus said, his voice a low growl. "They want us to chase them, to play their game. But we're not going to play by their rules."

Instead of chasing the mercenaries, Marcus and his team decided to go after the source. They knew that the mercenaries were just pawns in a larger game. They had to find the base, the hidden fortress where The Chimera was training their soldiers, planning their operations, building their army.

Kenji and Sarah launched a new digital hunt, a search for the hidden base. They sifted through satellite imagery, through shipping manifests, through encrypted communications. They were looking for a ghost, a hidden fortress that was not on any map.

They found it on a small, uninhabited island in the Aegean Sea, a rocky outcrop that was a perfect hiding place. It was a former military base, a relic of the Cold War that had been repurposed by The Chimera. It was a fortress, a training ground, a launchpad for their global operations.

"If we can take down their base," Marcus said, his voice a low command, "we can cut off their ability to launch these kinds of attacks. We can take away their army."

The plan was a daring one: a full-scale assault on the island, a battle that would be fought on The Chimera's home turf. It was a risky move, a high-stakes gamble. But the ghosts were not afraid of a fight.

They assembled a small fleet of unmarked boats, a team of ghosts who were about to launch their own private invasion. They approached the island under the cover of darkness, a team of shadows on a moonless sea. They were a force of nature, a team of hunters who were about to walk into the heart of darkness.

The Mediterranean assault was a battle of epic proportions, a clash of two armies of ghosts. The fighting was fierce, brutal, and bloody. The ghosts were outnumbered, but they were not outmatched. They were a team of warriors, a family of hunters who were fighting for the future of the world.

They fought their way to the heart of the base, a command center that was the nerve center of The Chimera's military operations. They were about to deliver a devastating blow to the enemy, a blow that would cripple their ability to wage war. The hunt was reaching its climax. And the ghosts were on the verge of a major victory.

The breakthrough came in the form of a single piece of intelligence, a thread that led them to the heart of The Chimera's operations. The brain, the central intelligence that was coordinating their attacks, was hidden in a fortress on a private island in the Mediterranean, a place that was known only as The Citadel.

The assault on The Citadel was a masterpiece of tactical planning, a coordinated attack that was designed to overwhelm the enemy's defenses. They came from the sea and the sky, a two-pronged assault that would catch The Chimera off guard.

The sea team, led by Marcus and Elena, approached the island in a fleet of small, fast boats. They were ghosts on the water, their movements a study in stealth and precision. They landed on a secluded beach, a small strip of black sand that was hidden from the fortress's surveillance.

The air team, led by Viktor and Anya, dropped from the sky in a HALO jump, a high-altitude, low-opening descent that was designed to avoid detection. They landed on the cliffs above the fortress, a vantage point that would allow them to provide cover for the ground assault.

The battle was fierce, a clash of two armies of ghosts. The Chimera's forces were well-trained, well-armed, and well-prepared. But they were not prepared for the fury of the Sterling team. The ghosts moved through the fortress like a whirlwind, their movements a symphony of violence and precision.

The Mediterranean assault was a turning point in the war, a decisive blow that would cripple The Chimera's operations. The hunt was reaching its climax. And the ghosts were closing in for the kill.

# Chapter 30: The Final Confrontation

The assault on the Mediterranean base was the turning point in the war against The Chimera. The battle was a brutal, hard-fought victory, a testament to the skill and the courage of Marcus and his team. They had destroyed The Chimera's military training facility, had captured a wealth of intelligence, and had sent a clear message to The Architect: the ghosts were coming for him.

The captured intelligence was a treasure trove, a map of The Chimera's global network, a list of their key operatives, a blueprint of their plans for a new world order. Kenji and Sarah worked around the clock, their fingers a blur on the keyboard as they sifted through the data, connecting the dots, painting a picture of an enemy that was more dangerous, more ambitious, more terrifying than they could have ever imagined.

They discovered the location of The Architect's main headquarters, a hidden fortress in the Swiss Alps, a place where he was building his shadow government, a place where he was planning his final move. He was planning a series of coordinated attacks on the world's financial markets, a digital Pearl Harbor that would plunge the global economy into chaos, a move that would allow him to seize control in the ensuing panic.

"He's planning to burn the world down so he can rule over the ashes," Marcus said, his voice a low growl. "We have to stop him. We have to stop him now."

The final confrontation was at hand. The ghosts were about to walk into the heart of darkness, to face The Architect in his own fortress, to fight a final battle for the future of the world.

They assembled their team for one last mission, a team of warriors who had been to hell and back together. They were a family, a band of brothers and sisters who were about to face their greatest challenge yet.

They traveled to Switzerland, a country of pristine beauty and hidden secrets. They moved through the mountains like a team of ghosts, their movements a study in coordinated precision. They were a force of nature, a team of hunters who were closing in on their prey.

They found the fortress, a high-tech marvel of engineering that was built into the side of a mountain. It was a modern-day castle, a fortress of security that was designed to be impenetrable. But the ghosts were masters of their craft. They were a team of hunters who could not be denied.

Javier found a way in, a weak point in the fortress's defenses. Anya led the way, a ghost in the shadows who moved with a silent grace. Marcus and Elena were the muscle, the warriors who were about to face The Architect and his army of ghosts.

The final confrontation was a battle of epic proportions, a clash of two ideologies, two visions for the future of the world. It was a battle between the old guard and the new, between the ghosts of the past and the architects of the future.

Marcus and his team fought their way to the heart of the fortress, a command center that was the nerve center of The Architect's shadow government. They were about to face the man who had tried to destroy them, the man who had threatened to burn the world to the ground. The final confrontation was at hand. And the fate of the world was hanging in the balance.

_md", text=

# ACT IV: THE FINAL RECKONING

The final confrontation took place in the heart of The Citadel, a grand chamber that was the nerve center of The Chimera's operations. It was a place of technology and terror, a space where the brain of the beast resided, where the orders were given, where the attacks were planned.

Marcus and his team fought their way to the chamber, a whirlwind of violence and chaos. The battle was a brutal, close-quarters affair, a dance of death in the corridors of the fortress. They were outnumbered, but they were not outmatched. They were a team of warriors, a family of hunters who were fighting for the future of the world.

They reached the chamber, a grand space that was filled with screens and servers, a digital throne room from which The Chimera had planned to rule the world. And in the center of it all, surrounded by a bank of monitors that showed the world teetering on the brink of chaos, was the man who called himself The Architect.

He was not what they had expected. He was not a monster, not a ghost, not a warrior. He was a man in a bespoke suit, a man with the calm, confident air of a CEO who was about to launch a new product. He was a man who believed in his vision, a man who was convinced that he was the hero of his own story.

"Phoenix," he said, his voice a low, calm murmur. "I've been expecting you."

"It's over, Architect," Marcus said, his voice a low growl. "Your plan has failed. Your army is gone. Your empire is crumbling."

The final confrontation was at hand. The heart of The Chimera had been reached. And the fate of the world was hanging in the balance.

# Chapter 31: The Battle in the Compound

The final battle was not a chaotic firefight, but a series of surgical strikes, a deadly game of chess played out in the sterile corridors of The Architect's fortress. Marcus and his team moved with the silent precision of ghosts, a force of nature that was dismantling The Chimera's defenses from the inside out.

Javier, with a grin that was a mixture of excitement and pure, unadulterated joy, disabled the fortress's internal security systems, plunging the compound into a state of controlled chaos. The guards were blind, their eyes and ears cut off, their high-tech fortress now a tomb.

Anya moved through the corridors like a phantom, a whisper of death in the shadows. She took out the elite guards with a brutal efficiency, her movements a symphony of violence that was as beautiful as it was terrifying. She was a ghost, a predator, a woman who was in her element.

Marcus and Elena moved as a single unit, a father-daughter team that was a force to be reckoned with. They were a whirlwind of motion, a blur of violence, a team of warriors who were fighting for their family, for their future, for the world. They were a testament to the blood that flowed in their veins, a legacy of warriors that would not be denied.

They fought their way to the command center, the heart of The Architect's shadow government. The room was a marvel of technology, a digital throne room from which The Architect had planned to rule the world. And in the center of it all, surrounded by a bank of monitors that showed the world teetering on the brink of chaos, was The Architect himself.

He was not what they had expected. He was not a monster, not a ghost, not a warrior. He was a man in a bespoke suit, a man with the calm, confident air of a CEO who was about to launch a new product. He was a man who believed in his vision, a man who was convinced that he was the hero of his own story.

"Phoenix," he said, his voice a low, calm murmur. "I've been expecting you."

"It's over, Architect," Marcus said, his voice a low growl. "Your plan has failed. Your army is gone. Your empire is crumbling."

"Is it?" The Architect replied, a faint smile on his face. "You've won a battle, Phoenix. But the war is far from over. The world is a chaotic, messy place. It needs a firm hand, a guiding vision. It needs an architect."

He was a true believer, a fanatic who was convinced that he was saving the world by burning it down. He was a man who could not be reasoned with, a man who had to be stopped.

The final confrontation was not a physical one, but a battle of wills, a clash of ideologies. Marcus, the warrior who had found his way back to the light, and The Architect, the visionary who had been consumed by the darkness. It was a battle for the soul of the world.

And in the end, it was not violence that won the day, but truth. Kenji and Sarah, the digital ghosts, had not only dismantled The Architect's network; they had also gathered the evidence, the proof of his crimes, the blueprint of his plan for a new world order. They broadcast it to the world, a digital truth bomb that exposed The Architect for what he was: a terrorist, a madman, a would-be dictator.

The world watched in stunned silence as the truth was revealed. The Architect's empire, built on a foundation of lies and manipulation, crumbled in an instant. The man who would be king was now a pariah, a ghost who had been exposed to the light.

He was a broken man, his vision shattered, his dream of a new world order in ruins. He was a ghost, a man with no future, no hope, no escape. The battle was over. The ghosts had won.

The battle in the compound was a symphony of violence, a coordinated assault that was designed to overwhelm the enemy's defenses. Marcus and his team moved through the fortress like a force of nature, their movements a study in controlled chaos.

Javier, with his expertise in explosives, created a series of diversions, controlled blasts that drew the guards away from the key positions. His work was a masterpiece of destruction, a testament to his skill and his nerve. He was a man who could turn chaos into an art form.

Anya moved through the corridors like a phantom, a whisper of death in the shadows. She took out the elite guards with a brutal efficiency, her movements a symphony of violence that was as beautiful as it was terrifying. She was a ghost, a predator, a woman who was in her element.

Viktor and Mei provided support from the flanks, a pair of warriors who were wreaking havoc on the ranks of the enemy. Viktor's brute strength was a counterpoint to Mei's surgical precision, a deadly duet that was tearing the compound apart.

Marcus and Elena were the spearhead, a father and daughter who were a force to be reckoned with. They fought their way to the command center, their movements a symphony of violence and precision. They were a team of warriors, a family of hunters who were fighting for the future of the world.

The battle was fierce, a clash of two armies of ghosts. The Chimera's forces were well-trained, well-armed, and well-prepared. But they were not prepared for the fury of the Sterling team. The compound was falling, the enemy was retreating, and the heart of The Chimera was within their reach.

# Chapter 32: The Long Road Home

The aftermath of the final battle was a strange and surreal experience. The Architect was in custody, his network was in shambles, and the world was slowly coming to terms with the scale of the threat that had been averted. The ghosts had won, had saved the world from a new kind of darkness. But the victory was a quiet one, a somber affair that was marked by a sense of profound exhaustion.

They left the Swiss Alps, a team of weary warriors who were finally, truly, going home. The journey back to Whidbey Island was a long and quiet one, a time for reflection, a time for healing. They had been to hell and back, had stared into the abyss, had been changed by what they had seen.

Marcus was a man at peace, a warrior who had finally found his way back to the light. He had faced the ghosts of his past, had confronted the darkness within himself, and had emerged victorious. He was no longer Phoenix, the ghost who walked in the shadows. He was Marcus Sterling, a husband, a father, a man who had found his purpose in the love of his family.

Elena was a young woman who had come into her own, a warrior who had found her place in the world. She was no longer a victim, no longer a survivor. She was a hero, a woman who had fought for the future, a woman who had helped to save the world. She was her father's daughter, a legacy of warriors that would continue for generations to come.

Tori was the anchor, the heart of the family, the woman who had stood by her husband through the darkest of times. She was a warrior in her own right, a woman of strength and courage who had faced the shadows without flinching. She was the reason Marcus had fought so hard, the reason he had found his way back to the light.

They returned to Whidbey Island, to their sanctuary, their home. The house was no longer a fortress, no longer a war room. It was a home, a place of peace, a place of love. The ghosts were gone, the shadows had been banished. The war was over.

The world was a different place, a world that had been changed by the war with The Chimera. The threat of a shadow government, of a private intelligence network that was more powerful than any government, was no longer a distant possibility. It was a real and present danger, a threat that had to be met with a new kind of vigilance, a new kind of courage.

The world needed heroes, a new generation of warriors who could walk in the shadows without being consumed by the darkness. The world needed a new kind of ghost, a new kind of hunter, a new kind of warrior.

And Marcus Sterling, the man who had been Phoenix, the man who had stared into the heart of darkness and had emerged victorious, knew that his work was not yet done. The war was over, but the battle for the future had just begun. And he and his family, his team, his ghosts, would be ready.

The journey home was a time of reflection, a period of quiet decompression after the intensity of the battle. The ghosts, no longer at war, had to learn to be at peace again. It was a transition that was as challenging as any battle they had fought.

They traveled in a military transport, a ghost plane that was invisible to radar, a shadow in the sky. The mood was somber, the air thick with the weight of the sacrifices that had been made. They had won, had saved the world from a new kind of darkness. But the victory was a costly one.

Marcus sat in the cargo hold, his eyes fixed on the darkness outside the window. He was a man at peace, a warrior who had finally found his way back to the light. He had faced the ghosts of his past, had confronted the darkness within himself, and had emerged victorious. He was no longer Phoenix, the ghost who walked in the shadows. He was Marcus Sterling, a husband, a father, a man who had found his purpose in the love of his family.

Elena sat beside him, her hand finding his in the darkness. She was a young woman who had come into her own, a warrior who had found her place in the world. She was no longer a victim, no longer a survivor. She was a hero, a woman who had fought for the future, a woman who had helped to save the world.

Tori was waiting for them when they landed, her presence a warmth that cut through the chill of the night. She was the anchor, the heart of the family, the woman who had stood by her husband through the darkest of times. She was a warrior in her own right, a woman of strength and courage who had faced the shadows without flinching.

The long road home was a journey of healing, a path that led them back to the light. The war was over. The ghosts had won. And now, they had a chance to build a new future.

# Chapter 33: Recovery and Reflection

The weeks following their return to Whidbey Island were a time of quiet decompression. The adrenaline of the hunt faded, replaced by a deep, bone-weary exhaustion. The ghosts, no longer at war, had to learn to be at peace again. It was a transition that was as challenging as any battle they had fought.

Javier and Anya stayed for a while, their presence a comforting reminder of the family they had forged in the crucible of combat. The boisterous energy of Javier and the quiet intensity of Anya filled the house, a lively counterpoint to the island's tranquility. They were a part of the Sterling family now, bound by a loyalty that transcended blood.

There were long evenings spent around the fire pit, the flames dancing against the backdrop of the star-filled sky. They shared stories, not of war and violence, but of their lives before the shadows, of the people they had been, the dreams they had held. It was a form of therapy, a way of reclaiming the parts of themselves that had been lost in the darkness.

Javier, with his infectious grin, told stories of his childhood in a small village in Colombia, of his fascination with fireworks that had led him down a very different, and much more explosive, career path. Anya, her usual reserve melting away in the warmth of the fire, spoke of her life in Tel Aviv, of the kibbutz where she had grown up, of the sense of duty that had led her to Mossad.

Marcus, in turn, shared stories of his own past, of a life before Phoenix, a life he had almost forgotten. He spoke of his parents, of his childhood, of the idealism that had led him to the CIA. He spoke of the man he had been, the man he was trying to be again.

Elena listened, her eyes a reflection of the fire's light. She was a young woman who was finally getting to know her father, the man behind the legend. She was seeing the cracks in the armor, the humanity beneath the warrior's façade. And she was loving him all the more for it.

Tori was the quiet center of these gatherings, her presence a source of warmth and stability. She was the one who had brought them all together, the one who had created this space of healing. She was the heart of their unconventional family.

Eventually, Javier and Anya had to leave, their own lives calling them back. Their departure left a void, a quiet that was both a relief and a source of sadness. The house felt a little emptier, a little quieter. But the bonds that had been forged remained, a network of loyalty and love that spanned the globe.

The period of recovery and reflection was a necessary one. It was a time for the ghosts to shed their skins, to remember who they were, to find their way back to the light. The war was over, but the journey of healing had just begun.

The weeks following their return to Whidbey Island were a time of quiet recovery. The adrenaline of the hunt faded, replaced by a deep, bone-weary exhaustion. The ghosts, no longer at war, had to learn to be at peace again. It was a transition that was as challenging as any battle they had fought.

The team scattered, returning to their own lives, their own families, their own futures. Viktor returned to Europe, where he was building a new life with a woman he had met during the mission. Mei returned to Asia, where she was using her skills to help victims of cyber crime. Omar returned to the Middle East, where he was working with a non-profit organization that helped refugees.

Javier and Anya stayed for a while, their presence a comforting reminder of the family they had forged in the crucible of combat. They were a part of the Sterling family now, bound by a loyalty that transcended borders and nationalities.

There were long evenings spent around the fire pit, the flames dancing against the backdrop of the star-filled sky. They shared stories, not of war and violence, but of their lives before the shadows, of the people they had been, the dreams they had held. It was a form of therapy, a way of reclaiming the parts of themselves that had been lost in the darkness.

The period of recovery and reflection was a necessary one. It was a time for the ghosts to shed their skins, to remember who they were, to find their way back to the light. The war was over, but the journey of healing had just begun.

# Chapter 34: A New Chapter

Life, after the storm, finds a new rhythm. For the Sterling family, the rhythm was one of purpose, of building something new from the ashes of their past. The idea had been planted in the fertile ground of their shared experience, a seed of a thought that had taken root and was now beginning to grow.

It was Elena who first gave it a voice. "We can't just go back to the way things were," she said one evening, as they sat on the deck, watching the sunset paint the sky in hues of orange and purple. "We have the skills, the experience, the network. We could do some good. On our own terms."

Marcus had been thinking the same thing. The world was a dangerous place, and the threats were not going to disappear just because The Chimera had been dismantled. There would always be new shadows, new ghosts, new architects of chaos. The government agencies, with their bureaucracy and their political constraints, were not always equipped to deal with these new threats. There was a need for a new kind of organization, a private entity that could operate with the speed and the agility of a ghost team, but with the moral compass of a group of people who had seen the darkness and had chosen the light.

"Sterling Global Solutions," Tori said, the name a sudden inspiration. "A private security firm. But not just any security firm. A firm that takes on the cases that no one else will touch, the ones that fall through the cracks. A firm that protects the innocent, that fights for justice, that makes a difference."

The idea was a powerful one, a way to channel their skills, their experience, their shared sense of purpose into something positive. It was a way to continue the fight, but on their own terms, by their own rules. It was a way to build a legacy, a legacy that was not defined by violence and destruction, but by protection and justice.

The decision was a unanimous one. They would build Sterling Global Solutions, a family business that was unlike any other. Marcus would be the strategist, the mastermind, the one who saw the big picture. Elena, with her lethal skills and her unwavering courage, would lead the field operations. Tori, with her business acumen and her people skills, would be the face of the organization, the one who managed the clients, the one who kept the books.

They reached out to their team, to the ghosts who were scattered across the globe. Javier, Anya, Kenji, and Sarah. They were all in, without a moment's hesitation. They were a family, a team, a group of warriors who were ready for a new chapter, a new mission.

The creation of Sterling Global Solutions was a new beginning, a new chapter in the story of the Sterling family. It was a way to turn their past into a source of strength, their scars into a symbol of their resilience. It was a way to build a future, a future where they were not just survivors, but protectors, guardians, a force for good in a world that was still filled with shadows.

Life, after the storm, finds a new rhythm. For the Sterling family, the rhythm was one of purpose, of building something new from the ashes of their past. The idea had been planted in the fertile ground of their shared experience, a seed of a thought that had taken root and was now beginning to grow.

It was Elena who first gave it a voice. "We can't just go back to the way things were," she said one evening, as they sat on the deck, watching the sunset paint the sky in hues of orange and purple. "We have the skills, the experience, the network. We could do some good. On our own terms."

Marcus had been thinking the same thing. The world was a dangerous place, and the threats were not going to disappear just because The Chimera had been dismantled. There would always be new shadows, new ghosts, new architects of chaos. The government agencies, with their bureaucracy and their political constraints, were not always equipped to deal with these new threats. There was a need for a new kind of organization, a private entity that could operate with the speed and the agility of a ghost team, but with the moral compass of a group of people who had seen the darkness and had chosen the light.

"Sterling Global Solutions," Tori said, the name a sudden inspiration. "A private security firm. But not just any security firm. A firm that takes on the cases that no one else will touch, the ones that fall through the cracks. A firm that protects the innocent, that fights for justice, that makes a difference."

The decision was a unanimous one. They would build Sterling Global Solutions, a family business that was unlike any other. A new chapter was beginning, a new adventure was about to unfold. And the Sterling family was ready.

# Chapter 35: The Gathering of Ghosts

The birth of Sterling Global Solutions was not a quiet affair. It was a gathering of ghosts, a reunion of warriors who had been scattered to the four corners of the earth. The house on Whidbey Island, once a sanctuary of peace, was once again a command center, a hive of activity, a place where a new kind of army was being born.

Javier arrived first, his grin as wide as the Colombian sky. He had left his teaching position without a second thought, the call to action a siren song he could not resist. He brought with him his expertise, his infectious energy, and a new set of toys, a collection of gadgets and explosives that made Marcus's eyebrows rise in a mixture of admiration and alarm.

Anya followed soon after, a silent shadow who appeared on their doorstep without a sound. She had left her life in Tel Aviv behind, her loyalty to the team a bond that was stronger than any national allegiance. She was a woman of few words, but her presence was a powerful one, a silent promise of the lethal skills she brought to the table.

Kenji and Sarah, the digital ghosts, were already there, their virtual presence a constant hum in the background. They had seamlessly integrated their cybersecurity firm with the new organization, their digital network now the backbone of Sterling Global Solutions. They were the eyes and ears, the digital guardians, the ones who would watch over the team as they walked into the shadows.

Colonel Jackson, true to his word, provided the support they needed. He couldn't officially sanction their activities, but he could provide them with intelligence, with resources, with the deniability they needed to operate in the gray areas of the world. He was a silent partner, a ghost in the machine, a man who understood that the world needed a team like Sterling Global Solutions.

The gathering of ghosts was a reunion of a family, a family that had been forged in the crucible of battle. They were a team of warriors, a band of brothers and sisters who had been to hell and back together. They were a force to be reckoned with, a team of specialists who were about to unleash their unique brand of justice on the world.

They spent the next few weeks in a whirlwind of planning and preparation. They converted the barn on the property into a state-of-the-art training facility, a place where they could hone their skills, test their new equipment, and prepare for the missions that lay ahead. They established a secure communications network, a digital fortress that was impenetrable to the outside world. They created a new set of protocols, a new way of operating, a new set of rules for a new kind of game.

Sterling Global Solutions was more than just a private security firm. It was a statement, a declaration of intent. It was a promise to the world that there was a new team of ghosts in town, a team that would fight for the innocent, that would protect the vulnerable, that would hunt the monsters that lurked in the shadows. The gathering of ghosts was over. The hunt was about to begin.

The birth of Sterling Global Solutions was not a quiet affair. It was a gathering of ghosts, a reunion of warriors who had been scattered to the four corners of the earth. The house on Whidbey Island, once a sanctuary of peace, was once again a command center, a hive of activity, a place where a new kind of army was being born.

Javier arrived first, his grin as wide as the Colombian sky. He had left his teaching position without a second thought, the call to action a siren song he could not resist. He brought with him his expertise, his infectious energy, and a new set of toys, a collection of gadgets and explosives that made Marcus's eyebrows rise in a mixture of admiration and alarm.

Anya followed soon after, a silent shadow who appeared on their doorstep without a sound. She had left her life in Tel Aviv behind, her loyalty to the team a bond that was stronger than any national allegiance. She was a woman of few words, but her presence was a powerful one, a silent promise of the lethal skills she brought to the table.

Kenji and Sarah, the digital ghosts, were already there, their virtual presence a constant hum in the background. They had seamlessly integrated their cybersecurity firm with the new organization, their digital network now the backbone of Sterling Global Solutions. They were the eyes and ears, the digital guardians, the ones who would watch over the team as they walked into the shadows.

Colonel Jackson, true to his word, provided the support they needed. He couldn't officially sanction their activities, but he could provide them with intelligence, with resources, with the deniability they needed to operate in the gray areas of the world. He was a silent partner, a ghost in the machine, a man who understood that the world needed a team like Sterling Global Solutions.

The gathering of ghosts was a reunion of a family, a family that had been forged in the crucible of battle. They were a team of warriors, a band of brothers and sisters who had been to hell and back together. They were a force to be reckoned with, a team of specialists who were about to unleash their unique brand of justice on the world.

# Chapter 36: Forging a New Path

Sterling Global Solutions didn't wait for trouble to find them; they went looking for it. Their first official mission was not a high-profile, government-sanctioned operation, but a quiet, pro-bono case that was a statement of their new purpose. It was a case that had fallen through the cracks, a cry for help that had been ignored by the authorities.

A young journalist, an American who had been investigating a human trafficking ring in Eastern Europe, had disappeared. The local police were calling it a missing person case, but her family knew better. They had received a ransom demand, a demand that was accompanied by a chilling photograph of their daughter, bruised and terrified. They had gone to the embassy, to the FBI, to anyone who would listen. But the wheels of bureaucracy turned slowly, and the trail was growing cold.

They came to Sterling Global Solutions as a last resort, a desperate plea for help. And the ghosts answered the call.

The mission was a classic Sterling operation: swift, silent, and brutally effective. Kenji and Sarah, with their digital wizardry, tracked the source of the ransom demand to a fortified compound in the mountains of Albania. It was a stronghold of a local crime syndicate, a place that was considered to be untouchable.

Marcus, Elena, Javier, and Anya went in, a team of ghosts who moved with the silent precision of a predator. The assault was a symphony of violence, a blur of motion in the dead of night. They dismantled the compound's defenses, took out the guards, and rescued the journalist, all without a single casualty on their side.

The rescue made headlines around the world. The story of the young journalist who had been saved by a mysterious, unnamed security firm was a sensation. The name Sterling Global Solutions was not mentioned, but the message was clear: there was a new player in the game, a new force for good in a world that was filled with shadows.

The success of their first mission brought them a new level of recognition, a new kind of currency in the world of shadows. They were no longer just a team of former operatives; they were a legend in the making, a group of ghosts who were earning a reputation for being the best in the business.

They took on more cases, each one a new challenge, a new opportunity to make a difference. They rescued a group of aid workers who had been taken hostage by a warlord in Africa. They exposed a corrupt politician who was selling state secrets to a foreign power. They dismantled a drug cartel that was terrorizing a small village in South America.

They were a force for good, a team of warriors who were using their skills to protect the innocent, to fight for justice, to make the world a safer place. They were forging a new path, a path that was defined not by their past, but by their future. They were a family, a team, a legacy. And their story was just beginning.

# Epilogue

Five years later, the world was a different place, and so was the Sterling family. Sterling Global Solutions had grown from a fledgling startup into one of the most respected and effective private security firms in the world. Their name was whispered in the corridors of power, a symbol of hope for those in need, a source of fear for those who lurked in the shadows.

Marcus, no longer a ghost, had fully embraced his role as the strategic mastermind of the organization. He was the chess master, the one who saw the patterns in the chaos, the one who guided his team through the most complex and dangerous missions. He had found a new kind of peace, a new sense of purpose, a new way to be a warrior.

Elena had become a legend in her own right, a field operative who was as brilliant as she was deadly. She led her team with a quiet confidence, a natural leader who had earned the respect and the loyalty of her soldiers. She was her father's daughter, a warrior who had found her own path, her own way to make a difference.

Tori was the heart and the soul of the organization, the one who kept the machine running. She was a brilliant businesswoman, a savvy negotiator, a compassionate leader. She was the one who made sure that Sterling Global Solutions never lost its moral compass, never forgot its true purpose.

They were a family, a team, a force for good in a world that was still filled with shadows. They had built a legacy, a legacy that was a testament to their resilience, their courage, their love.

One evening, as Marcus sat in his office, the command center of their global operations, he looked at the wall of monitors that showed the world in all its chaotic beauty. He saw his team in action, a group of ghosts who were fighting for a better future. He saw his daughter, a warrior who was leading her team with a grace and a courage that made his heart swell with pride. He saw his wife, a leader who was changing the world, one mission at a time.

He smiled, a genuine, heartfelt smile of a man who had found his way home. The journey had been a long and difficult one, a path that had been paved with pain and loss. But it had led him here, to this moment of peace, of purpose, of love.

A priority alert flashed on his screen, a new message from a new client, a new cry for help from a dark corner of the world. A new threat, a new challenge. A new adventure.

Marcus leaned forward, his eyes alight with a familiar fire. The war was over, but the hunt was eternal. And Phoenix, the warrior, the husband, the father, was ready for whatever came next.

---

Sterling Global Solutions didn't wait for trouble to find them; they went looking for it. Their first official mission was not a high-profile, government-sanctioned operation, but a quiet, pro-bono case that was a statement of their new purpose. It was a case that had fallen through the cracks, a cry for help that had been ignored by the authorities.

A young journalist, an American who had been investigating a human trafficking ring in Eastern Europe, had disappeared. The local police were calling it a missing person case, but her family knew better. They had received a ransom demand, a demand that was accompanied by a chilling photograph of their daughter, bruised and terrified. They had gone to the embassy, to the FBI, to anyone who would listen. But the wheels of bureaucracy turned slowly, and the trail was growing cold.

They came to Sterling Global Solutions as a last resort, a desperate plea for help. And the ghosts answered the call.

The mission was a classic Sterling operation: swift, silent, and brutally effective. Kenji and Sarah, with their digital wizardry, tracked the source of the ransom demand to a fortified compound in the mountains of Albania. It was a stronghold of a local crime syndicate, a place that was considered to be untouchable.

Marcus, Elena, Javier, and Anya went in, a team of ghosts who moved with the silent precision of a predator. The assault was a symphony of violence, a blur of motion in the dead of night. They dismantled the compound's defenses, took out the guards, and rescued the journalist, all without a single casualty on their side.

The rescue made headlines around the world. The story of the young journalist who had been saved by a mysterious, unnamed security firm was a sensation. The name Sterling Global Solutions was not mentioned, but the message was clear: there was a new player in the game, a new force for good in a world that was filled with shadows.

The success of their first mission brought them a new level of recognition, a new kind of currency in the world of shadows. They were no longer just a team of former operatives; they were a legend in the making, a group of ghosts who were earning a reputation for being the best in the business.

They took on more cases, each one a new challenge, a new opportunity to make a difference. They rescued a group of aid workers who had been taken hostage by a warlord in Africa. They exposed a corrupt politician who was selling state secrets to a foreign power. They dismantled a drug cartel that was terrorizing a small village in South America.

They were a force for good, a team of warriors who were using their skills to protect the innocent, to fight for justice, to make the world a safer place. They were forging a new path, a path that was defined not by their past, but by their future. They were a family, a team, a legacy. And their story was just beginning.

Five years later, the world was a different place, and so was the Sterling family. Sterling Global Solutions had grown from a fledgling startup into one of the most respected and effective private security firms in the world. Their name was whispered in the corridors of power, a symbol of hope for those in need, a source of fear for those who lurked in the shadows.

The headquarters of Sterling Global Solutions was no longer the house on Whidbey Island, but a state-of-the-art facility on the outskirts of Seattle. It was a fortress of technology and security, a place where the ghosts could plan their operations, train their teams, and coordinate their global network. But the house on the bluff remained their home, their sanctuary, the place where they returned to remember who they were.

Marcus, no longer a ghost, had fully embraced his role as the strategic mastermind of the organization. He was the chess master, the one who saw the patterns in the chaos, the one who guided his team through the most complex and dangerous missions. He had found a new kind of peace, a new sense of purpose, a new way to be a warrior.

Elena had become a legend in her own right, a field operative who was as brilliant as she was deadly. She led her team with a quiet confidence, a natural leader who had earned the respect and the loyalty of her soldiers. She was her father's daughter, a warrior who had found her own path, her own way to make a difference.

Tori was the heart and the soul of the organization, the one who kept the machine running. She was a brilliant businesswoman, a savvy negotiator, a compassionate leader. She was the one who made sure that Sterling Global Solutions never lost its moral compass, never forgot its true purpose.

They were a family, a team, a force for good in a world that was still filled with shadows. They had built a legacy, a legacy that was a testament to their resilience, their courage, their love.

One evening, as Marcus sat in his office, the command center of their global operations, he looked at the wall of monitors that showed the world in all its chaotic beauty. He saw his team in action, a group of ghosts who were fighting for a better future. He saw his daughter, a warrior who was leading her team with a grace and a courage that made his heart swell with pride. He saw his wife, a leader who was changing the world, one mission at a time.

He smiled, a genuine, heartfelt smile of a man who had found his way home. The journey had been a long and difficult one, a path that had been paved with pain and loss. But it had led him here, to this moment of peace, of purpose, of love.

A priority alert flashed on his screen, a new message from a new client, a new cry for help from a dark corner of the world. Marcus leaned forward, his eyes scanning the details. It was a complex case, a situation that would require all of their skills, all of their resources, all of their courage.

He reached for his phone, ready to assemble his team, ready to answer the call. But before he could dial, another message appeared on his screen, a priority alert from an old contact, a ghost from his past.

The message was simple, a single line of text that sent a chill down his spine: "The Architect has a successor. The game is not over."

Marcus stared at the screen, his mind a whirlwind of analysis. A new threat, a new challenge. A new adventure.

He looked out the window, at the sun setting over the Puget Sound, at the world that was still filled with shadows. He thought of his family, of his team, of the legacy they had built. He thought of the battles they had fought, the sacrifices they had made, the victories they had won.

And he smiled, a warrior's smile, a smile of a man who was ready for whatever came next.

"Let's go to work," he said, his voice a low command.

The hunt was eternal. And Phoenix, the warrior, the husband, the father, was ready.

---

The training of Elena Sterling was a process that began long before she joined her father's team. She had been forged in the crucible of her own tragic past, a young woman who had been shaped by violence and betrayal. But the training she received from Marcus was different. It was a training of the mind as much as the body, a process that was designed to turn her into a complete warrior.

They trained in the early morning hours, when the world was still and quiet, when the only sounds were the crash of the waves and the call of the seabirds. Marcus was a demanding teacher, a man who pushed her to her limits and then pushed her further. He taught her the art of combat, the science of tactics, the philosophy of war.

"Fighting is not about strength," he told her, his voice a low rumble. "It's about control. It's about knowing when to strike and when to wait. It's about understanding your enemy, anticipating their moves, exploiting their weaknesses."

She learned to fight with her hands, her feet, her elbows, her knees. She learned to use weapons, from knives to guns to improvised tools. She learned to move silently, to blend into the shadows, to become invisible. She was a natural, a woman who had been born to be a warrior.

But the training was not just physical. Marcus also taught her the mental aspects of combat, the psychology of war. He taught her to control her fear, to channel her anger, to stay calm under pressure. He taught her to think like a warrior, to see the world as a battlefield, to always be prepared for the unexpected.

"The mind is the most powerful weapon," he told her. "A warrior who can control their mind can control any situation. Fear is the enemy. Doubt is the enemy. The moment you let them in, you've already lost."

The training was grueling, exhausting, and sometimes painful. But Elena never complained, never faltered, never gave up. She was her father's daughter, a woman who was determined to prove herself, to earn her place at the table. And by the time the training was complete, she was ready. She was a warrior, a ghost, a Sterling.

The love story of Marcus and Tori Sterling was one that had been written in the stars, a romance that had survived the darkest of times. They had met years ago, when Marcus was still Phoenix, when he was still walking in the shadows. She had been a real estate agent, a woman who was building a life in the light. He had been a ghost, a man who was haunted by the things he had done.

Their meeting had been a chance encounter, a collision of two worlds that should never have intersected. But there had been something between them, a spark that had ignited a fire that could not be extinguished. She had seen past the mask, past the walls he had built, past the darkness that surrounded him. She had seen the man beneath, the man who was desperate to be loved, to be understood, to be saved.

"I knew you were dangerous the moment I met you," she told him once, her voice a soft whisper. "But I also knew you were worth the risk."

Their relationship had been a tumultuous one, a rollercoaster of passion and pain. There had been times when the shadows had threatened to consume them, when the secrets of his past had nearly torn them apart. But they had survived, had fought for each other, had built a love that was stronger than any enemy they had faced.

"You are my anchor," he told her, his voice a low rumble. "You are the reason I fight, the reason I come home, the reason I believe in a future. Without you, I would be lost in the darkness."

She was his light, his hope, his salvation. She was the woman who had saved him from himself, who had shown him that there was more to life than violence and death. She was the love of his life, the mother of his family, the heart of his home.

Their love story was one for the ages, a romance that had been forged in the fires of adversity. They had faced the shadows together, had fought the darkness side by side. And they had emerged, scarred but unbroken, a couple who had proven that love could conquer all.

The team that Marcus Sterling assembled was more than just a group of specialists. They were a brotherhood, a family of warriors who were bound by a loyalty that transcended borders, nationalities, and ideologies. They were a team of ghosts, a band of brothers and sisters who had been to hell and back together.

Javier, the explosives expert, was the heart of the team. He was a man of infectious energy, a warrior who could find humor in the darkest of situations. He was the one who kept morale high, who reminded them that they were fighting for something worth fighting for. He was a brother, a friend, a man who would die for any member of the team.

Anya, the former Mossad agent, was the silent guardian. She was a woman of few words, but her presence was a powerful one. She was the one who watched their backs, who protected them from the shadows. She was a sister, a warrior, a woman who was as loyal as she was lethal.

Kenji and Sarah, the digital ghosts, were the eyes and ears of the team. They were a pair of geniuses, a couple who had found love in the world of code and data. They were the ones who guided the team through the digital battlefield, who provided the intelligence that was the lifeblood of their operations. They were a part of the family, a vital organ in the body of the team.

The brotherhood of warriors was a bond that could not be broken, a loyalty that could not be bought. They were a team of ghosts, a family of hunters who were fighting for a better world. They were a force to be reckoned with, a group of specialists who were about to unleash their unique brand of justice on the world.

Marcus Sterling, the man who had been Phoenix, had developed a philosophy over his years of service, a set of principles that guided his actions, that defined his character. It was a philosophy that was born of experience, of the lessons he had learned in the darkest corners of the world.

"The world is not black and white," he told Elena once, as they sat on the deck, watching the sunset. "It's a thousand shades of gray. Good people do bad things. Bad people do good things. The line between hero and villain is thinner than you think."

He believed in the power of redemption, in the ability of people to change, to grow, to become better than they were. He had seen the worst of humanity, had witnessed the depths of depravity that people could sink to. But he had also seen the best, had witnessed acts of courage and sacrifice that had restored his faith in the human spirit.

"We are not defined by our past," he said. "We are defined by our choices, by the actions we take in the present. Every day is a chance to be better, to do better, to make a difference."

He believed in the importance of family, of the bonds that tied people together. He had spent years as a ghost, a man who was alone in the world, who had no one to fight for, no one to come home to. But Tori and Elena had changed that, had given him a reason to live, a reason to fight, a reason to believe in a future.

"Family is everything," he said. "It's the anchor that keeps us grounded, the light that guides us through the darkness. Without family, we are nothing."

The philosophy of Phoenix was a code, a set of principles that guided his actions, that defined his character. It was a philosophy that was born of pain and loss, of the lessons he had learned in the shadows. And it was a philosophy that he passed on to his daughter, a legacy that would endure long after he was gone.

The world of shadows was a place that existed beneath the surface of everyday life, a hidden realm where the rules of the normal world did not apply. It was a world of spies and assassins, of arms dealers and terrorists, of governments and criminal organizations that operated in the gray areas of morality.

Marcus Sterling had walked in this world for most of his adult life, had been a part of its machinery, had seen its darkest corners. He knew its rules, its players, its dangers. He knew that it was a world where trust was a currency that was always in short supply, where betrayal was a constant threat, where death was always just around the corner.

"The world of shadows is not a place for the faint of heart," he told Elena. "It's a place where the stakes are life and death, where the consequences of failure are catastrophic. It's a place where you have to be willing to do things that would horrify the people in the light."

But he also knew that the world of shadows was a necessary one, a place where the battles that could not be fought in the open were waged. It was a place where the threats that the normal world could not see were confronted, where the monsters that lurked in the darkness were hunted.

"We are the guardians of the light," he said. "We walk in the shadows so that others don't have to. We do the things that need to be done, the things that no one else is willing to do. We are the ghosts, the hunters, the warriors who stand between the darkness and the light."

The world of shadows was a dangerous place, a realm where the line between good and evil was often blurred. But it was also a place where heroes were born, where legends were made, where the fate of the world was decided. And Marcus Sterling, the man who had been Phoenix, was one of its greatest warriors.

The legacy of the Sterling family was one that would endure for generations, a story of courage, sacrifice, and love that would inspire those who came after. They were a family of warriors, a dynasty of ghosts who had dedicated their lives to protecting the innocent, to fighting for justice, to making the world a safer place.

Marcus Sterling was the patriarch, the founder, the man who had started it all. He was a legend, a warrior who had walked through the world's darkest corners and had emerged, scarred but unbroken. He was the one who had built Sterling Global Solutions, who had assembled the team, who had forged the family.

Tori Sterling was the heart, the soul, the anchor. She was the woman who had saved Marcus from himself, who had given him a reason to fight, a reason to believe in a future. She was the one who kept the family together, who reminded them of what they were fighting for.

Elena Sterling was the future, the heir, the next generation. She was a warrior in her own right, a woman who had earned her place at the table. She was the one who would carry on the legacy, who would lead the team when her father was gone, who would ensure that the Sterling name would endure.

The legacy of the Sterlings was a story that was still being written, a saga that would continue for generations to come. They were a family of warriors, a dynasty of ghosts, a force for good in a world that was still filled with shadows. And their story was far from over.

The future was a vast, uncharted territory, a landscape of possibilities that stretched out before the Sterling family like an endless horizon. They had faced the darkness, had fought the shadows, had emerged victorious. But they knew that the war was never truly over, that there would always be new threats, new challenges, new battles to fight.

Sterling Global Solutions was thriving, a beacon of hope in a world that was still filled with shadows. They had built a reputation, a legacy, a name that was synonymous with justice and protection. They were the ghosts, the hunters, the warriors who stood between the darkness and the light.

Marcus looked at his family, at the team he had assembled, at the legacy he had built. He saw Tori, the love of his life, the woman who had saved him from himself. He saw Elena, his daughter, a warrior who had found her own path. He saw Javier and Anya, Kenji and Sarah, the brothers and sisters who had become his family.

He thought of the battles they had fought, the sacrifices they had made, the victories they had won. He thought of the people they had saved, the lives they had changed, the difference they had made. He thought of the future, the challenges that lay ahead, the adventures that awaited.

And he smiled, a warrior's smile, a smile of a man who was ready for whatever came next.

The future awaited. And the Sterling family was ready.

Intelligence was the lifeblood of Sterling Global Solutions, the foundation upon which all of their operations were built. Without accurate, timely intelligence, even the most skilled warriors were blind, stumbling through the darkness without a guide. Marcus understood this better than anyone, having spent decades in a world where information was the most valuable currency.

Kenji and Sarah had built a digital empire, a network of sensors and algorithms that could sift through the vast ocean of data that flowed through the world's networks. They could track financial transactions, intercept communications, analyze patterns that were invisible to the human eye. They were the digital ghosts, the watchers in the machine, the ones who saw everything.

"Information is power," Kenji explained to Elena during one of their training sessions. "The more you know about your enemy, the more advantages you have. Their weaknesses, their habits, their fears. All of it can be used against them."

But intelligence was not just about data. It was also about human sources, the network of contacts and informants that Marcus had cultivated over a lifetime of service. These were the ghosts in the field, the eyes and ears on the ground, the people who could provide the kind of information that no algorithm could uncover.

"Technology is a tool," Marcus told her. "But it's not a replacement for human intelligence. The best information comes from people, from relationships, from trust. That's something that no computer can replicate."

The art of intelligence was a complex one, a blend of technology and human intuition, of data analysis and street smarts. It was the foundation of Sterling Global Solutions, the engine that powered their operations. And it was a skill that Elena was learning to master, a tool that would serve her well in the battles to come.

Combat was not just a physical endeavor; it was a psychological one as well. The mind was the most powerful weapon, and the warrior who could control their mind could control any situation. Marcus had learned this lesson early in his career, had seen how fear and doubt could paralyze even the most skilled fighters.

"Fear is natural," he told Elena during one of their training sessions. "It's a survival mechanism, a warning system that tells you when you're in danger. But you can't let it control you. You have to acknowledge it, accept it, and then push through it."

He taught her techniques for managing fear, for staying calm under pressure, for maintaining focus in the chaos of combat. He taught her to breathe, to center herself, to find the stillness within the storm. He taught her to visualize success, to see herself winning before the battle even began.

"The mind is like a muscle," he said. "The more you train it, the stronger it becomes. You have to practice staying calm, practice controlling your emotions, practice being in the moment. It's not something that comes naturally. It's something you have to work at."

The psychology of combat was a critical skill, one that separated the good warriors from the great ones. It was the ability to stay calm when everything was falling apart, to think clearly when the bullets were flying, to make the right decisions when lives were on the line. And it was a skill that Elena was determined to master.

The ethics of war was a topic that Marcus had grappled with throughout his career, a question that had no easy answers. In the world of shadows, the line between right and wrong was often blurred, the choices rarely clear-cut. He had done things that he was not proud of, had made decisions that haunted him to this day.

"War is not a clean business," he told Elena. "There are no good guys and bad guys, no heroes and villains. There are just people, making choices, trying to survive. Sometimes those choices are easy. Sometimes they're not."

He taught her to think about the consequences of her actions, to consider the impact of her decisions on the people around her. He taught her that every life had value, that every death was a tragedy, that violence should always be a last resort.

"We are not executioners," he said. "We are protectors. Our job is to save lives, not to take them. We use force when we have to, but we never enjoy it. We never forget that the people we're fighting are human beings, with families and dreams and fears."

The ethics of war was a complex topic, one that had no easy answers. But Marcus believed that it was important to think about these questions, to grapple with the moral implications of their work. He believed that a warrior who did not question their actions was a warrior who had lost their humanity.

Trust was the foundation of the Sterling team, the glue that held them together through the darkest of times. In the world of shadows, where betrayal was a constant threat, trust was a rare and precious commodity. It was something that had to be earned, something that had to be maintained, something that could be lost in an instant.

Marcus had learned the value of trust the hard way, had been betrayed by people he had considered friends, had seen the devastating consequences of misplaced faith. But he had also experienced the power of true trust, the strength that came from knowing that someone had your back, that they would die for you without hesitation.

"Trust is not given," he told Elena. "It's earned. It's built over time, through actions, through shared experiences. It's the result of proving yourself, of showing that you're reliable, that you're loyal, that you're willing to sacrifice for the team."

The bonds of trust within the Sterling team were forged in the crucible of combat, in the moments when they had to rely on each other to survive. They had seen each other at their best and their worst, had shared their fears and their hopes, had built a connection that was deeper than friendship.

"We are a family," Marcus said. "Not by blood, but by choice. We have chosen to trust each other, to fight for each other, to die for each other if necessary. That's what makes us strong. That's what makes us unbreakable."

Leadership was a skill that Marcus had honed over decades of service, a craft that he had learned through trial and error, through success and failure. He had led teams into the most dangerous situations imaginable, had made decisions that had determined the fate of nations. He knew what it took to be a leader, and he was determined to pass that knowledge on to Elena.

"Leadership is not about giving orders," he told her. "It's about inspiring people, about earning their respect, about making them want to follow you. It's about setting an example, about being the first one into the breach, about never asking your people to do something you wouldn't do yourself."

He taught her the importance of communication, of making sure that everyone on the team understood the mission, the objectives, the risks. He taught her the value of listening, of taking input from her team, of being open to new ideas. He taught her the necessity of making tough decisions, of being willing to take responsibility for the consequences.

"A leader is not perfect," he said. "A leader makes mistakes. But a leader owns those mistakes, learns from them, and moves forward. A leader does not blame others, does not make excuses, does not hide from the truth."

The art of leadership was a lifelong journey, a process of continuous learning and growth. Marcus had been a leader for most of his adult life, and he was still learning, still growing, still becoming better. And he knew that Elena had the potential to be an even greater leader than he was.

Freedom was not free. It was a truth that Marcus had learned early in his career, a lesson that had been written in blood and sacrifice. The world was a dangerous place, and there were forces that sought to destroy the freedoms that people took for granted. Someone had to stand against those forces, had to be willing to pay the price.

"We are the guardians of freedom," he told his team. "We stand in the gap, we hold the line, we fight the battles that others cannot fight. We do this not for glory, not for recognition, but because it is the right thing to do."

The price of freedom was measured in lives, in the sacrifices of the men and women who had given everything to protect the innocent. It was measured in the scars, both physical and psychological, that the warriors carried with them. It was measured in the relationships that were strained, the families that were separated, the normal lives that were never lived.

"We pay a price for what we do," Marcus said. "We sacrifice our peace, our comfort, our safety. We live in the shadows so that others can live in the light. It's a choice we make, a burden we carry, a price we pay willingly."

The price of freedom was high, but it was a price that the Sterling team was willing to pay. They were warriors, guardians, protectors. They were the ones who stood between the darkness and the light. And they would continue to fight, continue to sacrifice, continue to pay the price, for as long as it took.

The dawn of a new era was upon them, a time of change and transformation that would reshape the world of shadows. Sterling Global Solutions was at the forefront of this change, a beacon of hope in a world that was still filled with darkness. They were the pioneers, the trailblazers, the ones who were charting a new course.

The old ways were dying, the traditional structures of power and control crumbling under the weight of their own corruption. The governments, the intelligence agencies, the military organizations that had once dominated the world of shadows were struggling to adapt to a new reality. They were slow, bureaucratic, bound by rules and regulations that made them ineffective against the new threats.

Sterling Global Solutions was different. They were agile, flexible, unbound by the constraints that hampered the traditional organizations. They could move quickly, adapt to changing circumstances, take on missions that others could not. They were a new kind of organization, a hybrid of the old and the new, a model for what the future of security could look like.

"We are the future," Marcus told his team. "We are the ones who will shape the world of shadows for generations to come. We have a responsibility, a duty, to do this right. To build something that is not just effective, but ethical. Something that protects the innocent, that fights for justice, that makes the world a better place."

The dawn of a new era was a time of opportunity and challenge, a moment when the choices they made would determine the course of history. The Sterling team was ready, prepared to face whatever the future held. They were warriors, guardians, pioneers. And they were about to change the world.

At the heart of every warrior was a fire, a burning passion that drove them to fight, to sacrifice, to endure. It was a fire that could not be extinguished, a flame that burned even in the darkest of times. It was the heart of a warrior, the essence of what made them who they were.

Marcus Sterling had carried that fire for most of his adult life, a flame that had been kindled in the crucible of his early experiences and had grown stronger with each passing year. It was a fire that had driven him to become Phoenix, to walk in the shadows, to fight the battles that others could not fight.

"The heart of a warrior is not about strength or skill," he told Elena. "It's about purpose. It's about knowing why you fight, what you're fighting for, who you're fighting to protect. Without purpose, a warrior is just a weapon. With purpose, a warrior is a force for good."

Elena had inherited that fire from her father, a flame that burned in her own heart. She had found her purpose in the crucible of her own experiences, in the battles she had fought, in the people she had saved. She was a warrior, a guardian, a Sterling.

The heart of a warrior was the most powerful weapon of all, a force that could not be defeated, a flame that could not be extinguished. It was the essence of what made the Sterling team so formidable, the foundation upon which their legacy was built. And it was a fire that would continue to burn for generations to come.

Home was more than just a place; it was a sanctuary, a refuge from the chaos of the world. For the Sterling family, the house on Whidbey Island was that sanctuary, a place where they could shed the armor of their profession and simply be themselves.

The house had been transformed over the years, evolving from a simple beach cottage into a sprawling compound that reflected the family's unique needs. There was the main house, a warm and inviting space where the family gathered for meals and conversation. There was the guest house, a place where their extended family of warriors could stay when they visited. There was the training facility, a state-of-the-art gym where they honed their skills. And there was the command center, a secure room where they planned their operations.

But beneath all the technology and security, the house was still a home. It was a place of laughter and love, of quiet moments and shared memories. It was a place where Tori tended her garden, where Marcus read his books, where Elena practiced her yoga. It was a place where the ghosts could be human again.

"This is what we fight for," Marcus said one evening, as they sat on the deck, watching the sunset. "Not for glory, not for recognition, but for this. For the chance to have a home, a family, a life. For the chance to be at peace."

The sanctuary of home was the foundation of the Sterling family, the anchor that kept them grounded through the storms of their profession. It was a reminder of what they were fighting for, a beacon of light in a world of shadows.

Experience was the greatest teacher, a harsh but effective instructor that had shaped Marcus Sterling into the warrior he had become. He had learned his lessons in the field, in the crucible of combat, in the moments when life and death hung in the balance.

"Books can teach you theory," he told Elena. "Training can teach you technique. But experience teaches you wisdom. It teaches you what works and what doesn't, what matters and what doesn't, what's worth fighting for and what's not."

He shared his experiences with her, the stories of his missions, the lessons he had learned, the mistakes he had made. He told her about the times he had succeeded and the times he had failed, the victories that had been celebrated and the defeats that had been mourned. He told her about the people he had saved and the people he had lost, the friends who had died and the enemies who had been vanquished.

"Every mission is a lesson," he said. "Every battle is an opportunity to learn. The key is to pay attention, to reflect on what happened, to understand why things went the way they did. The warrior who stops learning is the warrior who stops growing."

The wisdom of experience was a treasure that Marcus was passing on to Elena, a legacy of knowledge that would serve her well in the battles to come. It was the accumulated wisdom of a lifetime of service, a gift from a father to his daughter.

Resilience was the quality that separated the survivors from the victims, the warriors who endured from those who broke. It was the ability to take a hit and keep going, to fall down and get back up, to face adversity and emerge stronger.

The Sterling family had resilience in abundance, a quality that had been forged in the fires of their experiences. They had faced the worst that the world could throw at them and had emerged, scarred but unbroken. They had lost friends and loved ones, had suffered injuries and setbacks, had experienced failures and disappointments. But they had never given up, never surrendered, never stopped fighting.

"Resilience is not about being invincible," Marcus told Elena. "It's about being able to recover. It's about having the mental and emotional strength to bounce back from adversity. It's about refusing to let the hard times define you."

He taught her techniques for building resilience, for developing the mental toughness that would carry her through the darkest of times. He taught her to focus on what she could control, to accept what she couldn't, to find meaning in the struggle. He taught her to lean on her family, to draw strength from the bonds they shared, to never face the darkness alone.

"We are stronger together," he said. "That's the secret of our resilience. We support each other, we lift each other up, we carry each other through the hard times. That's what family is for."

Duty was a concept that had guided Marcus Sterling throughout his career, a sense of obligation that had driven him to serve, to sacrifice, to fight. It was a call that he could not ignore, a voice that spoke to him in the quiet moments, a force that compelled him to action.

"Duty is not about orders," he told Elena. "It's not about following commands or obeying rules. It's about a sense of responsibility, a feeling that you have an obligation to do something, to make a difference, to serve a cause greater than yourself."

He had felt the call of duty from a young age, a sense that he was meant for something more than an ordinary life. He had answered that call by joining the military, by becoming a special operator, by walking in the shadows. He had served his country, had protected the innocent, had fought the enemies of freedom.

"The call of duty never goes away," he said. "Even now, even after all these years, I still feel it. I still feel the pull, the need to serve, the desire to make a difference. It's a part of who I am, a part of who we are."

The call of duty was a powerful force, one that had shaped the Sterling family and would continue to shape them for generations to come. It was the foundation of their legacy, the essence of their purpose, the heart of their identity.

Tomorrow was a promise, a hope, a dream of a better future. For the Sterling family, tomorrow was the reason they fought, the goal they strived for, the vision that guided their actions.

"We fight for tomorrow," Marcus said. "We fight so that our children and our children's children can live in a world that is safer, freer, better. We fight so that the darkness does not consume the light, so that hope is not extinguished, so that the future is not lost."

The promise of tomorrow was a powerful motivator, a force that drove the Sterling team to push through the pain, to endure the hardships, to make the sacrifices. It was a vision of a world where the shadows were held at bay, where the innocent were protected, where justice prevailed.

"We may not see that world in our lifetime," Marcus said. "But we can help build it. We can lay the foundation, we can plant the seeds, we can pave the way. We can make the world a little bit better, a little bit safer, a little bit brighter. And that's worth fighting for."

The promise of tomorrow was the ultimate goal of Sterling Global Solutions, the vision that guided their mission, the dream that inspired their actions. It was a promise that they were determined to keep, a future that they were committed to building.

The eternal flame was a symbol of the Sterling legacy, a fire that would burn for generations to come. It was a flame that had been kindled by Marcus, nurtured by Tori, and would be carried forward by Elena. It was a flame that represented their values, their principles, their commitment to making the world a better place.

"This flame is our legacy," Marcus said, as they gathered around the fire pit on a cool evening. "It represents everything we stand for, everything we fight for, everything we believe in. It's a reminder of who we are and what we're capable of."

The eternal flame was more than just a symbol; it was a living testament to the Sterling family's dedication to their cause. It was a fire that burned in their hearts, a passion that drove their actions, a light that guided their way.

"We are the keepers of the flame," Elena said, her voice a fierce determination. "We are the ones who will carry it forward, who will pass it on to the next generation, who will ensure that it never goes out."

The eternal flame was the heart of the Sterling legacy, a fire that would burn for eternity. It was a symbol of hope, of courage, of love. It was a promise that the Sterling family would always be there, always fighting, always protecting, always making a difference.

And as the flames danced in the darkness, casting their warm glow on the faces of the Sterling family, Marcus smiled. He had found his purpose, his peace, his home. He had built a legacy that would endure, a family that would carry on, a flame that would never be extinguished.

The story of the Sterling family was far from over. It was just beginning.

And the future was bright.

Sterling Global Solutions did not operate in isolation. Over the years, they had built a network of allies, a web of relationships that spanned the globe. These were the contacts, the informants, the partners who provided the support that made their operations possible.

Colonel Jackson remained their most valuable ally in the government, a man who understood the value of what they did and was willing to provide the support they needed. He could not officially sanction their activities, but he could provide intelligence, resources, and the political cover that allowed them to operate in the gray areas.

There were others as well. A former MI6 agent who ran a private intelligence firm in London. A retired Mossad officer who had built a security consulting business in Tel Aviv. A former French Foreign Legion commander who operated a training facility in Morocco. These were the allies who formed the backbone of their network, the partners who could be called upon when the situation demanded.

"No one can do this alone," Marcus told Elena. "We need allies, partners, friends. We need people who share our values, who understand our mission, who are willing to stand with us when the darkness comes."

The network of allies was a force multiplier, a way of extending their reach and their capabilities. It was a testament to the relationships that Marcus had built over a lifetime of service, a legacy of trust and cooperation that would serve the Sterling family well in the battles to come.

Not every battle was fought with weapons. Sometimes, the most important victories were won at the negotiating table, through the art of persuasion and compromise. Marcus had learned this lesson early in his career, had seen how a well-placed word could be more powerful than a bullet.

"Negotiation is a form of combat," he told Elena. "It's a battle of wills, a contest of strategy and tactics. The goal is to achieve your objectives while minimizing the cost. Sometimes that means fighting. Sometimes that means talking."

He taught her the principles of negotiation, the techniques that could be used to influence and persuade. He taught her to listen, to understand the other side's perspective, to find the common ground that could lead to agreement. He taught her to be patient, to be flexible, to be willing to compromise when necessary.

"The best negotiators are the ones who can see the situation from the other side's point of view," he said. "They understand what the other side wants, what they fear, what they're willing to give up. They use that understanding to craft a deal that works for everyone."

The art of negotiation was a valuable skill, one that would serve Elena well in her role as a leader. It was a tool that could be used to resolve conflicts, to build alliances, to achieve objectives without resorting to violence. And it was a skill that she was determined to master.

Command was a heavy burden, a weight that rested on the shoulders of those who led. It was the responsibility for the lives of the people under your command, the accountability for the decisions you made, the pressure of knowing that your choices could mean the difference between life and death.

Marcus had carried that weight for most of his adult life, had felt the crushing pressure of command in the most dangerous situations imaginable. He had made decisions that had saved lives and decisions that had cost them. He had experienced the triumph of victory and the agony of defeat. He knew what it meant to lead.

"Command is not a privilege," he told Elena. "It's a responsibility. It's the burden of knowing that people are counting on you, that their lives are in your hands. It's the weight of making decisions when there are no good options, when every choice has consequences."

He taught her to embrace the weight of command, to accept the responsibility that came with leadership. He taught her to make decisions quickly and decisively, to trust her instincts, to learn from her mistakes. He taught her to care for her people, to put their welfare above her own, to never forget that they were human beings with families and dreams.

"The best leaders are the ones who feel the weight of command most heavily," he said. "They're the ones who take their responsibility seriously, who never forget that lives are at stake, who always strive to do better."

Mentorship was a sacred bond, a relationship between teacher and student that was built on trust, respect, and a shared commitment to growth. Marcus had been both a mentor and a student throughout his career, had learned from the best and had passed that knowledge on to the next generation.

His relationship with Elena was the most important mentorship of his life, a bond between father and daughter that was also a bond between master and apprentice. He was teaching her everything he knew, sharing the wisdom of a lifetime of experience, preparing her to carry on the Sterling legacy.

"A mentor is not just a teacher," he told her. "A mentor is a guide, a counselor, a friend. A mentor is someone who believes in you, who pushes you to be better, who is there for you when you fall. A mentor is someone who sees your potential and helps you realize it."

Elena had embraced the mentorship, had absorbed the lessons with a hunger that made Marcus proud. She was a quick learner, a natural warrior, a woman who was destined for greatness. She was the future of the Sterling legacy, the one who would carry the torch when he was gone.

"One day, you will be the mentor," he told her. "You will pass on what you have learned to the next generation. That's how the legacy continues. That's how the flame keeps burning."

Unity was the strength of the Sterling team, the force that made them greater than the sum of their parts. They were a diverse group, a collection of individuals from different backgrounds, different cultures, different experiences. But they were united by a common purpose, a shared commitment to making the world a better place.

"We are stronger together," Marcus said. "That's not just a slogan. It's a truth. When we work together, when we support each other, when we combine our strengths, we become unstoppable."

The strength of unity was evident in every operation they conducted, in the seamless coordination of their movements, in the way they anticipated each other's actions, in the trust they placed in each other.

They were a team, a family, a force.

Javier's explosives expertise complemented Anya's infiltration skills. Kenji's digital wizardry supported Viktor's tactical acumen. Mei's cyber capabilities enhanced Omar's ground intelligence. And Marcus and Elena, father and daughter, were the heart of the team, the leaders who brought everyone together.

"Unity is not about being the same," Marcus said. "It's about respecting our differences, leveraging our unique strengths, working together toward a common goal. It's about recognizing that we need each other, that we're better together than we are apart."

The strength of unity was the foundation of Sterling Global Solutions, the secret of their success, the key to their future. It was a strength that would carry them through the challenges ahead, a force that would make them unstoppable.

The journey of the Sterling family was a never-ending one, a path that stretched out before them like an endless horizon. They had come so far, had overcome so much, had built something that was truly remarkable. But they knew that the journey was not over, that there were still battles to fight, still challenges to face, still adventures to be had.

Marcus looked at his family, at the team he had assembled, at the legacy he had built. He saw Tori, the love of his life, the woman who had saved him from himself. He saw Elena, his daughter, a warrior who had found her own path. He saw Javier and Anya, Kenji and Sarah, Viktor and Mei and Omar, the brothers and sisters who had become his family.

He thought of the battles they had fought, the sacrifices they had made, the victories they had won. He thought of the people they had saved, the lives they had changed, the difference they had made. He thought of the future, the challenges that lay ahead, the adventures that awaited.

And he smiled, a warrior's smile, a smile of a man who was ready for whatever came next.

The journey continued. The story was far from over. And the Sterling family was ready.

Ready to fight. Ready to protect. Ready to make a difference.

Ready for the next adventure.

The end... for now.

The first official client of Sterling Global Solutions was not a government agency or a multinational corporation. It was a small non-profit organization that worked to protect endangered wildlife in Africa. They had been targeted by a sophisticated poaching syndicate, their rangers murdered, their sanctuaries violated, their mission threatened.

The case was not glamorous, and it would not pay well. But it was exactly the kind of mission that Sterling Global Solutions had been created for. It was a chance to make a difference, to protect the innocent, to fight for a cause that mattered.

"This is who we are," Marcus told his team. "We don't just take the high-profile cases, the ones that pay the big money. We take the cases that matter, the ones where we can make a real difference. This is our first mission, and it's going to set the tone for everything that follows."

The operation was a masterpiece of planning and execution. Kenji and Sarah tracked the poaching syndicate's communications, mapping their network and identifying their leadership. Javier and Anya infiltrated their base of operations, gathering intelligence and planting surveillance devices. Viktor and Mei coordinated with local authorities, building a coalition of support.

And when the time came, Marcus and Elena led the assault, a surgical strike that dismantled the syndicate and brought its leaders to justice. The operation was a complete success, a victory that saved countless animals and protected the brave rangers who had dedicated their lives to conservation.

The first client was a statement of purpose, a declaration of the values that would guide Sterling Global Solutions. They were not just a security firm; they were a force for good, a team of warriors who were committed to making the world a better place.

Word spread quickly in the world of shadows. Sterling Global Solutions had arrived, and they were not to be underestimated. Their reputation grew with each successful mission, each case solved, each client protected.

They took on a variety of cases, each one a new challenge, a new opportunity to prove themselves. They protected a whistleblower who had exposed corruption in a major pharmaceutical company. They rescued a group of hostages who had been taken by a terrorist cell in the Middle East. They dismantled a human trafficking ring that had been operating across three continents.

Each mission was a testament to their skills, their dedication, their commitment to their cause. They were a team of professionals, a family of warriors who were earning a reputation for being the best in the business.

"We're not just building a company," Tori said. "We're building a legacy. We're creating something that will outlast us, something that will continue to make a difference long after we're gone."

The reputation of Sterling Global Solutions was their most valuable asset, a currency that opened doors and created opportunities. It was a reputation that had been earned through hard work, sacrifice, and an unwavering commitment to their values.

As Sterling Global Solutions grew, so did the need for new talent. Marcus and Elena developed a training program, a rigorous course of instruction that was designed to identify and develop the next generation of warriors.

The program was not for the faint of heart. It was a grueling regimen of physical training, tactical instruction, and psychological conditioning. It was designed to push candidates to their limits, to test their resolve, to separate the wheat from the chaff.

"We're not looking for soldiers," Marcus told the candidates. "We're looking for warriors. There's a difference. A soldier follows orders. A warrior thinks for themselves. A soldier fights because they're told to. A warrior fights because they believe in something."

The training program produced a new generation of Sterling operatives, men and women who had been forged in the crucible of the program and had emerged as true warriors. They were the future of Sterling Global Solutions, the ones who would carry on the legacy when the founders were gone.

Sterling Global Solutions expanded its operations across the globe, establishing a network of offices and operatives that spanned six continents. They had a presence in every major city, a team of specialists who could respond to any crisis, anywhere in the world.

The global network was a force multiplier, a way of extending their reach and their capabilities. It allowed them to take on cases that would have been impossible for a smaller organization, to coordinate operations across multiple time zones, to leverage local knowledge and resources.

"We're not just a company anymore," Elena said. "We're a movement. We're a global force for good, a network of warriors who are committed to making the world a safer place."

The global network was the culmination of years of hard work and dedication, a testament to the vision that Marcus and Tori had shared from the beginning. It was a legacy that would endure for generations, a force that would continue to fight the darkness long after the founders were gone.

The Sterling family grew over the years, not just in numbers but in depth and connection. Javier married a woman he had met during a mission in Colombia, a doctor who had been working with refugees. Anya found love with a former Israeli intelligence officer who had joined the Sterling team. Kenji and Sarah had their first child, a daughter they named Hope.

The family gatherings at the house on Whidbey Island became legendary, a celebration of the bonds that had been forged in the crucible of combat. There was laughter and music, stories and memories, a warmth that cut through the chill of the Pacific Northwest.

"This is what we fight for," Marcus said, as he looked around at the faces of his family. "Not for glory, not for recognition, but for this. For the chance to have a family, to be surrounded by people who love us, to build something that matters."

The family was the heart of Sterling Global Solutions, the foundation upon which everything else was built. It was a family that had been forged in the fires of adversity, a family that had grown stronger with each passing year.

Elena Sterling was no longer just a member of the team; she was a leader in her own right. She had grown into her role, had developed her skills, had earned the respect of everyone who worked with her. She was the future of Sterling Global Solutions, the one who would carry on the legacy when her father stepped aside.

"You're ready," Marcus told her one evening, as they sat on the deck, watching the sunset. "You've learned everything I can teach you. You've proven yourself in the field. You've earned the trust of the team. It's time for you to take the lead."

Elena felt the weight of the responsibility, the enormity of what her father was asking. But she also felt the fire in her heart, the passion that drove her to fight, to protect, to make a difference. She was a Sterling, a warrior, a leader.

"I won't let you down," she said, her voice a fierce determination. "I'll carry on the legacy. I'll make you proud."

The next generation was ready. The torch was being passed. And the future of Sterling Global Solutions was in good hands.

Marcus Sterling, the man who had been Phoenix, found peace in his sunset years. He stepped back from the day-to-day operations of Sterling Global Solutions, content to serve as an advisor, a mentor, a wise elder who was always there when needed.

He spent his days with Tori, the love of his life, the woman who had saved him from himself. They traveled the world together, visiting the places they had always wanted to see, making memories that would last a lifetime. They returned to Whidbey Island often, to the house on the bluff, to the sanctuary they had built together.

"I never thought I would have this," Marcus said one evening, as they sat on the deck, watching the sunset. "I never thought I would live long enough to grow old, to have a family, to find peace. But here I am, surrounded by the people I love, doing work that matters. It's more than I ever dreamed of."

The sunset years were a time of reflection and gratitude, a period of quiet contentment after a lifetime of struggle. Marcus had found his peace, his purpose, his home. He had built a legacy that would endure, a family that would carry on, a flame that would never be extinguished.

And as the sun set over the Puget Sound, painting the sky in hues of orange and purple, Marcus Sterling smiled. He was a warrior who had found his peace. He was a ghost who had come home. He was a man who had lived a life worth living.

And the story continued.

Sterling Global Solutions was at the forefront of security technology, always seeking new tools and techniques that could give them an edge in the field. Kenji and Sarah led the technology division, a team of engineers and programmers who were constantly innovating, constantly pushing the boundaries of what was possible.

They developed advanced surveillance systems that could track targets across multiple platforms, from satellite imagery to social media. They created secure communication networks that were impervious to interception, allowing the team to coordinate operations in real-time. They built predictive algorithms that could anticipate threats before they materialized, giving the team a crucial head start.

"Technology is a force multiplier," Kenji explained. "It allows us to do more with less, to see further, to move faster. But it's not a replacement for human judgment. The best technology in the world is useless without the right people to use it."

The technology of tomorrow was a key component of Sterling Global Solutions' success, a tool that enhanced their capabilities and extended their reach. It was a testament to the innovation and creativity of the team, a reflection of their commitment to staying ahead of the curve.

Sterling Global Solutions operated according to a strict code of honor, a set of principles that guided their actions and defined their character. It was a code that had been developed by Marcus, refined by the team, and embraced by everyone who wore the Sterling badge.

The code was simple but profound:

Protect the innocent. Fight for justice. Never abandon a teammate. Honor your word. Respect your enemies. Learn from your mistakes. Serve a cause greater than yourself.

"The code is not just a set of rules," Marcus told the team. "It's a way of life. It's a commitment to being the best version of ourselves, to holding ourselves to a higher standard, to never compromising our values."

The code of honor was the moral compass of Sterling Global Solutions, the foundation upon which their reputation was built. It was a code that set them apart from the mercenaries and the criminals who operated in the world of shadows, a code that made them true warriors.

The bonds of brotherhood within the Sterling team were forged in the crucible of combat, in the moments when they had to rely on each other to survive. They were bonds that transcended nationality, race, religion, and background. They were bonds that made them a family.

Javier, the Colombian explosives expert, had become like a brother to Marcus. They had fought side by side in a dozen countries, had saved each other's lives more times than they could count. Their friendship was a testament to the power of shared experience, the way that combat could forge connections that lasted a lifetime.

Anya, the Israeli assassin, had become like a sister to Elena. They had trained together, fought together, grown together. Their bond was a reflection of the way that women warriors could support and empower each other, the way that sisterhood could be as powerful as brotherhood.

"We are a family," Marcus said. "Not by blood, but by choice. We have chosen to stand together, to fight together, to die for each other if necessary. That's what makes us strong. That's what makes us unbreakable."

The bonds of brotherhood were the heart of Sterling Global Solutions, the force that made them greater than the sum of their parts. They were a family of warriors, a band of brothers and sisters who would stand together until the end.

The legacy of Sterling Global Solutions was one that would endure for generations, a story of courage, sacrifice, and love that would inspire those who came after. It was a legacy that had been built by Marcus and Tori, nurtured by Elena, and carried forward by the entire team.

The legacy was not just about the missions they had completed, the lives they had saved, the enemies they had defeated. It was about the values they had upheld, the principles they had defended, the example they had set. It was about showing the world that there was another way, that security and ethics were not mutually exclusive, that warriors could also be heroes.

"Our legacy is not what we do," Marcus said. "It's who we are. It's the values we live by, the principles we fight for, the example we set. Our legacy is the impact we have on the world, the difference we make in the lives of others."

The legacy of Sterling Global Solutions was a beacon of hope in a world that was still filled with shadows. It was a reminder that there were people who were willing to fight for what was right, who were committed to making the world a better place. It was a legacy that would endure for generations, a flame that would never be extinguished.

As the story of Shadows of War comes to a close, there is one final message that the Sterling family wants to share with the world. It is a message of hope, of courage, of love. It is a message that has been written in the blood and sacrifice of warriors, in the tears and laughter of families, in the quiet moments of reflection and the loud moments of celebration.

The message is simple:

The darkness is real. The shadows are everywhere. The threats are constant and ever-evolving. But so is the light. So is the hope. So is the courage of those who are willing to stand against the darkness.

We are the guardians of the light. We are the hunters in the shadows. We are the warriors who stand between the darkness and the innocent. We are the ones who fight so that others don't have to.

And we will never stop. We will never surrender. We will never give up.

Because the world needs us. Because the innocent need us. Because the future needs us.

We are Sterling Global Solutions. We are a family of warriors. We are a force for good.

And our story is just beginning.

---

*To be continued in Book Three: Shadows of Redemption*

The house on Whidbey Island had become more than just a home; it had become a sanctuary, a place of healing and renewal for the warriors who had given so much in service to others. The property had expanded over the years, growing from a simple beach cottage into a sprawling compound that served multiple purposes.

The main house remained the heart of the property, a warm and inviting space where the Sterling family gathered for meals, celebrations, and quiet moments of connection. The kitchen was always filled with the aroma of Tori's cooking, a blend of comfort food and international cuisine that reflected the diverse backgrounds of the team. The living room was a place of laughter and conversation, where stories were shared and memories were made.

The guest houses dotted the property, providing accommodation for the extended family of warriors who came and went. Each house was named after a fallen comrade, a tribute to those who had given their lives in service. There was the Jackson House, named after a teammate who had died in Afghanistan. The Petrov House, named after a Russian defector who had sacrificed himself to save the team. The Chen House, named after a Chinese-American operative who had been killed in action.

The training facility was a state-of-the-art complex that included a gym, a shooting range, a tactical simulation center, and a medical clinic. It was a place where the team honed their skills, where new recruits were trained, where injuries were treated and bodies were rehabilitated.

The command center was the nerve center of Sterling Global Solutions, a secure facility that was equipped with the latest technology. It was a place where operations were planned, intelligence was analyzed, and the global network was coordinated. It was a place where the ghosts did their work.

But perhaps the most important part of the property was the memorial garden, a quiet space that was dedicated to those who had fallen. It was a place of reflection and remembrance, where the team could honor their fallen comrades and find peace in the midst of their grief.

The Whidbey Island sanctuary was a testament to the values of the Sterling family, a physical manifestation of their commitment to each other and to their cause. It was a place of healing and renewal, a sanctuary in a world of shadows.

Surveillance was a critical component of Sterling Global Solutions' operations, a skill that required patience, precision, and a deep understanding of human behavior. The team had developed a sophisticated approach to surveillance that combined traditional techniques with cutting-edge technology.

Physical surveillance was the foundation, the art of watching and following targets without being detected. It required a blend of skills: the ability to blend into any environment, the patience to wait for hours without moving, the awareness to notice the smallest details. It was a skill that was honed through years of practice, a craft that was passed down from mentor to student.

Electronic surveillance was the force multiplier, the technology that extended the team's reach and capabilities. Kenji and Sarah had developed a suite of tools that could intercept communications, track movements, and gather intelligence from a distance. They could hack into security systems, monitor social media, and analyze patterns of behavior that revealed hidden connections.

"Surveillance is not just about watching," Marcus explained to Elena. "It's about understanding. It's about seeing the patterns, the connections, the relationships. It's about knowing your target better than they know themselves."

The art of surveillance was a critical skill for any operative, a tool that could mean the difference between success and failure. It was a skill that required both technical expertise and human intuition, a blend of science and art that was at the heart of Sterling Global Solutions' success.

Understanding the enemy was a critical component of Sterling Global Solutions' approach to security. They did not just study the tactics and capabilities of their adversaries; they studied their psychology, their motivations, their fears and desires.

"Every enemy has a story," Marcus told his team. "They have a reason for what they do, a motivation that drives them. If you can understand that motivation, you can predict their behavior. You can anticipate their moves. You can find their weaknesses."

The team developed psychological profiles of their adversaries, detailed analyses that explored their backgrounds, their beliefs, their patterns of behavior. They studied the leaders of criminal organizations, the masterminds behind terrorist plots, the corrupt officials who enabled the darkness to flourish.

"The most dangerous enemies are the ones who believe they are right," Marcus said. "They are the true believers, the ones who are willing to die for their cause. They are the hardest to defeat because they are not motivated by money or power, but by ideology."

The psychology of the enemy was a critical tool in the Sterling arsenal, a way of understanding the darkness that they fought against. It was a tool that allowed them to anticipate threats, to exploit weaknesses, to defeat adversaries who might otherwise be invincible.

Intelligence was the lifeblood of Sterling Global Solutions, the foundation upon which all of their operations were built. Without accurate, timely intelligence, even the most skilled warriors were blind, stumbling through the darkness without a guide.

The team had developed a sophisticated intelligence apparatus, a network of sources and methods that could gather information from anywhere in the world. They had human sources, informants and contacts who provided the kind of information that no technology could uncover. They had technical sources, the digital tools and surveillance systems that could intercept communications and track movements. They had open sources, the publicly available information that could reveal hidden patterns and connections.

"Intelligence is not just about gathering information," Kenji explained. "It's about analyzing it, understanding it, turning it into actionable knowledge. The best intelligence in the world is useless if you don't know what to do with it."

The importance of intelligence could not be overstated. It was the difference between success and failure, between life and death. It was the tool that allowed Sterling Global Solutions to stay one step ahead of their adversaries, to anticipate threats before they materialized, to protect the innocent from the darkness.

The future of security was a topic that Marcus and his team thought about often, a question that shaped their strategy and their investments. The world was changing rapidly, and the threats were evolving with it. Sterling Global Solutions had to stay ahead of the curve, had to anticipate the challenges of tomorrow.

"The future of security is not just about technology," Marcus said. "It's about people. It's about building teams of skilled, dedicated professionals who can adapt to any situation. It's about developing the next generation of warriors who will carry on the fight."

The team invested heavily in training and development, in building a pipeline of talent that would ensure the future of the organization. They recruited from the best military and intelligence units in the world, seeking out individuals who had the skills, the character, and the commitment to join the Sterling family.

They also invested in technology, in the tools and systems that would give them an edge in the battles to come. They developed artificial intelligence systems that could analyze vast amounts of data, identifying patterns and threats that would be invisible to human analysts. They created autonomous systems that could operate in environments too dangerous for humans. They built secure communication networks that could withstand the most sophisticated attacks.

The future of security was a challenge that Sterling Global Solutions was determined to meet, a mission that would require all of their skills, all of their resources, all of their dedication. They were the guardians of the light, the hunters in the shadows. And they would be ready for whatever the future held.

Every member of Sterling Global Solutions lived by a warrior's creed, a set of principles that defined their character and guided their actions. It was a creed that had been developed by Marcus, refined by the team, and embraced by everyone who wore the Sterling badge.

The creed was recited at the beginning of every mission, a reminder of who they were and what they stood for:

*I am a warrior, a guardian of the light.*

*I stand between the darkness and the innocent.*

*I fight not for glory, but for justice.*

*I protect those who cannot protect themselves.*

*I never abandon my teammates.*

*I honor my word and respect my enemies.*

*I learn from my mistakes and grow stronger.*

*I serve a cause greater than myself.*

*I am a Sterling. I am a ghost. I am a force for good.*

The warrior's creed was more than just words; it was a way of life. It was a commitment to excellence, to honor, to service. It was a reminder that they were part of something larger than themselves, a legacy that would endure for generations.

At the heart of the Sterling family was love, the force that bound them together through the darkest of times. It was a love that had been tested by fire, that had survived betrayal and loss, that had grown stronger with each passing year.

The love between Marcus and Tori was the foundation, a romance that had begun in the shadows and had blossomed into a partnership that was the envy of all who knew them. They had faced the darkness together, had fought for each other, had built a life that was filled with meaning and purpose.

The love between Marcus and Elena was a bond that had been forged in the crucible of their shared experiences. He had missed her childhood, had been absent during the years when she needed him most. But they had found each other, had built a relationship that was as strong as any father and daughter could hope for.

The love within the team was a brotherhood and sisterhood that transcended the boundaries of family. They were warriors who had fought together, who had bled together, who had saved each other's lives. They were a family in every sense of the word.

"Love is the most powerful force in the universe," Marcus said. "It's what gives us the strength to fight, the courage to sacrifice, the will to endure. Without love, we are just soldiers. With love, we are warriors."

Peace was the ultimate goal of Sterling Global Solutions, the dream that drove their every action. They fought not because they loved war, but because they loved peace. They walked in the shadows so that others could live in the light.

"We are not warriors because we enjoy violence," Marcus told his team. "We are warriors because we believe in peace. We fight so that others don't have to. We sacrifice so that others can live in safety. We walk in the darkness so that the light can shine."

The promise of peace was a vision of a world where the innocent were protected, where justice prevailed, where the darkness was held at bay. It was a vision that might never be fully realized, but it was a vision worth fighting for.

"Peace is not the absence of conflict," Marcus said. "It's the presence of justice. It's a world where people can live without fear, where children can grow up in safety, where families can thrive. That's what we fight for. That's what we sacrifice for. That's what we believe in."

The promise of peace was the North Star of Sterling Global Solutions, the guiding light that illuminated their path. It was a promise that they were determined to keep, a future that they were committed to building.

As the sun set over Whidbey Island, casting long shadows across the water, the Sterling family gathered on the deck of their home. They had been through so much together, had faced the darkness and had emerged, scarred but unbroken. They had built something remarkable, a legacy that would endure for generations.

Marcus looked at his family, at the team he had assembled, at the life he had built. He saw Tori, the love of his life, the woman who had saved him from himself. He saw Elena, his daughter, a warrior who had found her own path. He saw Javier and Anya, Kenji and Sarah, the brothers and sisters who had become his family.

He thought of the battles they had fought, the sacrifices they had made, the victories they had won. He thought of the people they had saved, the lives they had changed, the difference they had made. He thought of the future, the challenges that lay ahead, the adventures that awaited.

And he smiled, a warrior's smile, a smile of a man who was at peace.

"This is not the end," he said, his voice a low rumble. "This is just the beginning. We have built something remarkable, something that will endure. But our work is not done. The world still needs us. The innocent still need us. The future still needs us."

He raised his glass, a toast to the family he loved, to the team he led, to the legacy they had built.

"To Sterling Global Solutions," he said. "To the ghosts who walk in the shadows. To the warriors who fight for the light. To the family that will never be broken."

The glasses clinked, the laughter rang out, and the sun dipped below the horizon, painting the sky in hues of orange and purple.

The end of one chapter. The beginning of another.

www.ingramcontent.com/pod-product-compliance
Lightning Source LLC
Chambersburg PA
CBHW060646260626
47161CB00008B/3014